ONE DOWN

Two Bears hurled himself at Hawk. Hawk took a quick step to one side, caught the Indian's arm, and threw him through the air. The massive Blackfoot landed stunned on his back.

Hawk fitted an arrow into Two Bears' bow. "This arrow will bury itself in your heart unless you tell what happened to my sister," Hawk said.

"One man—a trapper—stole her." Two Bears' eyes went mean and small. "We were busy with your whore of a sister and did not see him come up."

"You are a dangerous enemy, Two Bears. But I would have let you go if you had not said that," Hawk said. He lifted the bow almost casually and let the arrow fly.

Hawk barely glanced at the Indian choking on his own blood. He was already planning his next step on the vengenace trail. . . .

DOUBLE BARRELED ACTION!

GOLDEN HAWK #8

CAPTIVE'S TRAIL

Will C. Knott

A SIGNET BOOK

NEW AMERICAN LIBRARY

PUBLISHER'S NOTE

This book is a work of fiction. Names, characters, places, and incidents either are the product of the author's imagination or are used fictitiously, and any resemblance to actual persons, living or dead, events, or locales is entirely coincidental.

NAL BOOKS ARE AVAILABLE AT QUANTITY DISCOUNTS WHEN USED TO PROMOTE PRODUCTS OR SERVICES. FOR INFORMATION PLEASE WRITE TO PREMIUM MARKETING DIVISION, NEW AMERICAN LIBRARY, 1633 BROADWAY, NEW YORK, NEW YORK 10019.

SIGNET TRADEMARK REG. U.S. PAT. OFF. AND FOREIGN COUNTRIES
REGISTERED TRADEMARK—MARCA REGISTRADA
HECHO EN CHICAGO, U.S.A.

SIGNET, SIGNET CLASSIC, MENTOR, ONYX, PLUME, MERIDIAN and NAL BOOKS are published by NAL PENGUIN INC., 1633 Broadway, New York, New York 10019

First Printing, June, 1988

1 2 3 4 5 6 7 8 9

PRINTED IN THE UNITED STATES OF AMERICA

GOLDEN HAWK

A quiet stream under the Comanche moon . . . leaping savages . . . knives flashing in the firelight . . . brutal, shameful death . . .

Ripped from the bosom of their slain parents and carried off by the raiding Comanches, Jed Thompson and his sister can never forget that hellish night under the glare of the Comanche moon, seared into their memories forever.

Years later, his vengeance slaked, pursued relentlessly by his past Comanche brothers, Jed is now Golden Hawk. Half Comanche, half white man. A legend in his time, an awesome nemesis to some—a bulwark and a refuge to any man or woman lost in the terror of that raw, savage land.

— 1 —

Hawk paused and held his hand up to warn Tames Horses. The old warrior hadn't needed Hawk's warning. He had frozen in midstride, his ancient face lifted, his head turned slightly as the distant sounds of a struggle came to them through the tangle of underbrush.

"Grizzly," whispered Hawk.

It was maybe poking into a bee's nest for its honey. Either that or it was plundering a camp. The sounds were coming from off to his right.

Tames Horses nodded solemnly. "The Beast Who Walks Like a Man. Yes. Maybe be better we go in other direction. This time of year, they feed for winter. Get big as young buffalo."

Still crouching warily, Hawk nodded. Then they heard a terrible, flaming oath, followed by the bear's shattering response—a roar that seemed to shake the forest. With silence and discretion no longer a consideration, the two men changed direction and plunged toward the commotion, coming out a moment later into a small clearing.

One glanced told Hawk everything.

A partially demolished tepee stood in the clearing,

one side completely torn open, the tanned buffalo-hide cover ripped like paper. To one side of the tepee a half-dozen pelts hung on stretched willow hoops, drying, the flesh side turned to face the sun. These were untouched. But a trail of destruction led from the tepee's gaping hole past the racks of beaver pelts to a dense patch of underbrush on the far side of the clearing. From there came the enraged woofs and snarls of the infuriated beast as it tore at whatever had aroused its fury, more than likely the Indian whose tepee it had been disturbed looting.

Checking his Hawken's load, Hawk moved swiftly but cautiously toward the sounds of struggle. Tames Horses kept pace with him, his white hair moving in the breeze like tufts of cotton. He held his bow out in front of him, an arrow's notch already fitted to the bowstring. A muffled but powerful shot came from the tangle of underbrush. It sounded like a flintlock pistol of some ancient variety, and the immediate result was an increase in the volume of the grizzly's rage.

Hawk's foot came down on a dry branch. The snap echoed in the enclosed clearing like a rifle shot and a second later a fearfully wounded bear tore from the brush to face them. The handle of a long, buffalo knife protruded from its shoulder, the blood from the blade already matting its chest, and one side of its muzzle had just been blown away, more blood seeping over the clean white exposed bone of its mangled lower jaw.

All this damage only seemed to endow the beast with a supernatural fury and strength as it reared up with a roar, standing a full eight feet tall—then charged. Its lumbering gate, though appearing slow to the eye, enabled the huge beast to close with Hawk and Tames

Horses with startling speed. As Tames Horses poured arrow after arrow into the onrushing animal, Hawk stood his ground, lifted the crescent-shaped butt of the half-stock to his shoulder, and placed his sights on the huge beast's massive chest.

By this time the grizzly was less than twenty feet away. Hawk fired point-blank, placing his ball into the great bear's heart. As he saw the hole appear in the animal's chest beside the shaft of one of Tames Horses' arrows, he became uncomfortably aware that no animal was harder to bring down and that one swipe of its taloned paw could rip him open from sole to crown.

But this bear was fashioned of flesh and blood, after all.

The huge beast pulled up and reared, swaying like a sailor on a pitching deck, one paw held up, as if to call a halt to the whole business. Its massive chest and shoulders resembled a bloody pincushion. Then, incredibly, the brute recovered and, with a fierce, guttural growl, came on again.

Cursing, Hawk poured powder down the rifle barrel and followed it with a lead ball, while Tames Horses, now on one knee beside him, kept fitting arrows to his bow and sending them at the bear. The infuriated beast woofed unhappily with each new arrow's arrival, and by the time Hawk had finished seating the load in his Hawken, it was close enough for him to see the bear's smashed teeth and gums, and its red, lolling tongue still remarkably intact.

Hawk lifted his Hawken and fired, this time the ball entered one of the bear's eye sockets and blew away half of its brain, the back of its skull exploding behind it in a pink cloud. The grizzly gave another loud bellow, then stopped, head lowered, its whole body swaying. Tames Horses spoke softly, reverently in Nez Percé and lowered his bow as a fresh stream of bright-red blood spurted from the bear's shattered muzzle.

The grizzly toppled over.

Hawk stood motionless in the clearing, aware that he was breathing hard. Then, reloading his rifle deliberately, he approached the huge bear with caution, poking gingerly at the beast's head with the rifle's muzzle. Tames Horses went down on one knee beside it, then looked up at Hawk and nodded in relief. The bear was finally dead.

They heard a sound and turned. A man Hawk had never seen before stepped from the brush. It was his hand that had buried the knife in the grizzly's chest and it was the bullet from his flintlock pistol that had torn away the grizzly's lower jaw. His right arm was streaming blood and his chest was crimson with it. A peeled flap of torn flesh combined with the front of his buckskin shirt. The side of his head was bleeding from ragged lacerations left by the grizzly's teeth.

The mountain man had taken a fearful mauling, and the wonder of it was that he was still on his feet.

He was tall and powerful of build, with broad, heavy shoulders, a barrel chest, and arms like small tree trunks. His long, powerful thighs were tightly encased in leggings of soft deerskin. His jacket, one that reached clear to his knees and was now fearfully torn about the chest and shoulders, was fringed along the shoulder and arm seams. It was dark with his sweat, animal fat, blood, and smoke. He wore thick, double-sole moccasins of buffalo hide, similar to Hawk's, which enabled him to walk soundlessly on the needle-covered floor of the forest or on dew-wet grass.

Under a round, wolfskin cap, his hair, snarled and

matted now with fresh blood, was a dark brown and reached clear to his shoulders. His beard, shaded from chocolate to rust red, was as long and as tangled as his hair. The visible facial skin covering his forehead and cheekbones and the powerful bridge of his nose was tanned to the shade of old leather; his eyes were two narrow slits of bright blue.

He blinked at them in some confusion as he strode crookedly into the clearing, holding his flintlock pistol in one hand. "Who are you two?" he asked, his voice low but harsh.

"My name's Thompson," Hawk replied. "Jed Thompson. This here Nez Percé is Tames Horses. And who might you be, friend?"

"Name's Gar Trimm," he mumbled, brushing past them.

"Where you bound?"

"Fort Hall," he responded, continuing toward his torn-up lodge. "Got some plews to trade. Damn grizzly might've tore them up."

"You alone?"

"Nope," he muttered without looking back at them, his voice a kind of low, guttural bark. "Got me a woman."

Hawk and Tames Horses followed Trimm to the nearly destroyed tepee, and when they reached it, they stood back out of respect for the man's feelings as he stepped through the torn hole in his tepee and bent over what the grizzly had left of his woman. She was an Arapaho and had been wrapped in furs when the grizzly attacked. There was some fool notion abroad that a sleeping human was safe from attack by the great bears, but here was evidence to the contrary. In death she looked up at them, her patient black-cherry eyes open wide in surprise. A few merciless swipes of the beast's talons had laid open, not only the furs she had wrapped about herself, but her olive skin from her shoulder to her thigh. Three ribs, resembling grotesque tusks, gleamed whitely as they protruded from the bloody wound.

Hawk watched the mountain man as he peered down at the dead woman. For an instant only he saw in the man's eyes a flicker of mild interest—a slight, barely perceptible nudge of grief. And that was all. It was as if death was this man's constant companion, a presence he accepted as easily as the wind in the pines over his head or the howl of winter storms about his lodge at night.

Turning from the dead woman, Trimm began an inspection of the damage the grizzly had done to his provisions and plews. Much of the jerked meat had been eaten, and the bear had found and ripped open two of Trimm's pressed and rawhide-bound packs of dried beaver plews. Cooking utensils and other gear were scattered about, but that was about the extent of the damage to his goods.

Noting the mountain man's apparent dismissal of his dead woman, Hawk shuddered inwardly, as if an icy hand had closed about his heart. It was immediately apparent to him that this lone, powerful man had become, over the years of his isolation in these wild mountains, similar in temperament to the wild beast they had just brought down—like the grizzly, he was simply a dumb brute who walked upright.

Reaching for one of the ripped-open packs of beaver plews, Trimm slipped to one knee, then keeled over slowly, coming to rest on his back, his face as pale as a sheet, his eyes closed. He was losing blood steadily from his wounds, and to this insult the man's powerful constitution had finally succumbed.

Tames Horses glanced at Hawk. "He is strong man. But maybe he need us to help him."

Hawk beside Trimm to examine his chest wounds. They were far more extensive than Hawk had guessed at first glance. One of the bear's talons had reached the man's left lung. Hawk looked up at Tames Horses and nodded in agreement.

"Looks like we better take him to the fort. There's a doctor there."

"White man's doctor?" Tames Horses shrugged. It was plain he didn't think much of the idea, but he wasn't going to argue the matter.

They found a shovel among the mountain man's gear and dug with it a shallow grave on a slight rise on the other side of the clearing, and in that buried the Arapaho woman. With night approaching, they built a fire, bound the man's wounds to stem the flow of blood, and waited through the night before starting for Fort Hall.

A week later, Hawk and Tames Horses rode out of the timbered foothills and started across the long, spring-fed flat that fronted Fort Hall. The mountain man, barely conscious, was tied onto the saddle of his large gray. Hawk and Tames Horses were leading Gar's two packhorses along with three packhorses of their own.

Hawk and Tames Horses had managed to rescue nearly 180 whole beaver plews from the grizzly's depradations. One of Trimm's packhorses carried two full packs of pelts, weighing close to one hundred pounds each. Gar's second packhorse was burdened with the remainder of the good pelts along with his traps, spare parts, cooking utensils, and other gear. Luckily, no more than thirty of the beaver skins had been so badly torn that they had to be discarded, those having been the pelts on top of the tightly pressed packs the grizzly had pawed. Tames Horses and Hawk surmised that Gar's haul of beaver pelts represented both his fall and spring trapping.

Since the day after his battle with the grizzly, Gar Trimm had been suffering from a raging fever. At times the fever had turned him into a terrible fury difficult to tie down, and it was Hawk's belief that, had the man been less of a giant, he would long since have died. For the past three days, however, he had been quieter, and the fever—though still constant—had subsided somewhat and he now appeared to be breathing without pain.

But despite Gar's giant constitution, the mountain man still needed bed rest and care—and perhaps a more thorough cleansing of his wounds.

This was what was on Hawk's mind as he and Tames Horses approached Fort Hall's gate, riding past a score or more of Crow Indian lodges ranging along the fort's western palisade. A shout came from the fort's entrance, and glancing up, Hawk saw Joe Meek riding out to meet them, his dark, round face wreathed in a wide grin.

Leaving Tames Horses to bring along Gar Trimm, Hawk urged his horse on ahead and met Joe Meek in front of the gate. Both men flung themselves off their horses and embraced.

"This child has a letter for you," Joe Meek cried.

A letter! Hawk realized it could be from only one person—Annabelle. Snatching the envelope from the grinning Joe Meek, he ripped it open and read the letter inside. When he finished, he looked up at Joe in despair.

"My God, Joe! She wrote this months ago. She should be here by now."

"That's why I rode out to meet you. Where you been, hoss? I been lookin' all over for you and that damn redskin. I got word a week ago from the child who brought this letter. They were expecting a steamboat a week after he left Fort Union. I'm thinkin' she's already left there herself, coming up the Yellowstone, maybe with a load of freight."

Hawk read the letter again, this time more carefully, savoring the sight of his sister's handwriting, the sound of her voice coming to him internally as he read her words. Annabelle's husband, Captain James Merriwether, was in Washington, busy on a government commission from the War Department. He had been selected to outfit an expedition whose charge was to find safer routes over the mountains to Oregon. Annabelle had insisted on going on ahead of him to visit with Jed, so distasteful to her had become Washington D.C., which—as she described it—was "filled with simpering females, mud, and mosquitoes."

He folded the letter and put it in his pocket, then waited with Joe Meek for Tames Horses and Trimm to reach the gate. As they did so, Hawk explained to Joe how they had come upon the wounded mountain man, assuring him that as soon as Trimm was taken care of, he would be moving out and heading north along the Yellowstone.

He would start that night, if possible.

— 2 —

The steamboat that Annabelle took to Fort Union did
not have an easy time. It was called the *Assiniboin*,
and was the successor to the first steamboat to make it
up the Missouri to Fort Union, the *Yellow Stone*. A
little more shallow of draft than that first steamboat,
the *Assiniboin* was over 120 feet long, twenty feet
abeam, and drew a little less than four feet of water
when substantially loaded. Her two side-wheels, more
than eighteen feet in diameter, were driven by powerful,
single-cylinder engines fed by steam from three boilers.

She had a crew of two dozen men, and throughout
the trip from St. Louis, nearly a hundred *engagés* slept
on the main deck. These French speaking employees
of the American Fur Company were no threat at all to
Annabelle. Indeed, so polite were they that whenever
she approached, they scrambled to their feet or pushed
away from the deck's railing to doff their stocking caps
in greeting. She knew they were only trying to be
polite, but the sight of their flashing white teeth, doffed
caps, and quick bows always made her feel self-conscious,
so that she tried not to walk too often on the main
deck, content to remain on the upper deck.

It was from there that she got a bird's-eye view of the crew's incredible exertions throughout the interminable voyage. For one thing, the Missouri's current was fierce and unpredictable. Sandbars appeared with unimaginable swiftness, rising before the steamboat's prow like the shifting shoulders of some subterranean being. The creaking, agonized sound of the hull grinding onto such bars would send Annabelle bolt upright in her bunk. It sounded as if something living were being tormented beyond its endurance, and she wondered at such times why the boat didn't simply break in two or why the brown, turgid waters of the Missouri did not smash through the hull and drown all of them in their bunks.

One afternoon, in order to rock the boat free of a sand bar's grip, the men on the ship ran in unison from one side to the other until the boat slid off into the current. The snags that formed when whole trees slid into the stream and became embedded in the sand were incredible hazards that twice nearly succeeded in punching holes in the steamboat's shallow hull.

Annabelle heard the ship's engineer complain to the captain once that the three fireboxes consumed at least ten cords of wood a day, an appetite so voracious that the ship's crewmen and the *engagés* on board were kept busy almost daily scavenging for the firewood needed to keep the engines going. Whenever the steamboat nosed over to the bank for a wood stop, she watched in amazement as the men swarmed ashore, axes in hand, and started cutting. If there was no dry, long-burning hardwood available, the men took the softer cottonwood and willow, and when that gave out, they turned to scrubby cedar. There were times when they were reduced to gathering up the driftwood that had piled up along the shores, and if it was still wet, the firemen tending the boilers would prime it with resin to make it burn.

In the company of Captain Smithers, Annebelle and three other passengers were taken on a tour of the hold. It was a fascinating experience. In the black, close hold the odor of newly hewn white oak timbers mingled with the homely, country-store aromas of flour casks, barrels of molasses, and boxes and bales that held everything the frontiersmen and trappers could want: rifles and powder, lead for casting into balls, bright fabrics, warm trade blankets, and iron pots for cooking.

For the Indian trade there were the inevitable, carefully stored barrels of whiskey sloshing heavily with each roll of the ship. In addition to the whiskey there were the beads and other trinkets and baubles designed to fascinate the savage Indian heart. With a sharp sense of recognition, Annabelle noticed as well the boxes of tiny, tinkling silver bells the Indian women would sew into the seams of their husband's leggings and shirts—and the needles, awls, knives, papers of pins, and pots of vermilion and other rouges to paint the Indian woman or her warrior's face and chest in preparation for battle.

Meanwhile, the nearer Annabelle got to Fort Union, the more rapid became her heartbeat. She was returning home. And this awareness filled her with a conflicting set of emotions: a strange, deep welling joy on the one hand, a stark and awful terror on the other. This wild, buffalo-carpeted wilderness through which they passed brought back to her memories of her lost babe and an anguish she could not choke down. She imagined she could feel his little hands clasping her aching breasts, his tiny mouth fastening about her rigid nipples. At such times she groaned inwardly and thought once more of the fine warrior who had been her husband and sired her son. In her mind's eye she could see the swarming Crow warriors galloping through her village, striking down its Shoshone defenders with terrible finality, and could feel again the icy river waters rushing over her, pulling her along as she swam for safety.

And, oddly enough, she began thinking also of her Comanche father, Buffalo Hump, and his woman Hank-of-Hair. For some reason her thoughts returned again and again to that old woman's wrinkled face, her quick movements, and the way she had of vetoing Buffalo Hump's whims with a sharp glance from her button-black eyes. Annabelle had never thought of Hank-of-Hair as her mother. For some reason they had never gotten along. Buffalo Hump had shown Annabelle too much partiality over the years and it was impossible for Hank-of-Hair not to notice it—and resent it.

The hot smell of the land, the sun-baked grasses especially, brought it all back to her, at times causing the fair hair on the back of her arms to rise in recognition. Lifting her head into the wind, she found she could smell distant Indian encampments, marked by the unmistakable aroma of dried buffalo hides. The smell of Indian seemed to fill the universe, and yet when she looked about her at the other passengers, they appeared to be aware only of their own immediate presence and their foolish, idle chatter.

They lacked entirely her own visceral sense of what this land represented—the wild openness of the high prairies and the hint of danger and savagery that hung on each shift of the breeze, each sign of smoke on the distant horizon, each small party of beribboned Indians racing along the river's banks, doing their best to keep up with this magical, smoke-belching monster.

What warmed her now was the certainty that Jed would be waiting for her at Fort Union, that his powerful arms would close about her, his face beaming. During the years after Buffalo Hump's sale of her to the Comancheros, she had known her brother would come for her. It was this—and this alone—that had sustained her.

And he had not disappointed her.

Now, as the steamboat labored upstream, crunching over sandbars or creeping through narrow channels, her impatience to see her brother became almost unbearable. It was difficult for her to believe how much she had looked forward to this visit. Though she hadn't mentioned it to Hawk in her letter, it was James's hope that Jed would accept the position of chief scout and share the leadership of his expedition with him. If Jed would accept such a commission, it would make Annabelle's happiness complete.

And why wouldn't he accept the offer? After all, it would be a glorious opportunity for them both. It might even make her brother and her handsome husband famous.

On one fine golden afternoon, she saw from the upper deck the treeless valley between two ranges of low bluffs through which the Missouri flowed, and on the shore overlooking it, near the mouth of the Yellow Stone River, sat Fort Union, the American Fur Company's most famous trading post.

Beside her on the deck stood Brad Balfour, a tall,

strapping fellow in his late twenties who had befriended her. He was handsome enough, with flaxen hair, blue eyes, and a solid chin. But despite his age, he seemed to Annabelle more like an overgrown boy or an affectionate puppy than a mature man. It was his innocence about the world that made her think of him this way; that, and the fact that he was filled with the most outlandish and foolish ideas, most of which he seemed to have acquired from books rather than from the world of real people.

He proclaimed himself eager to spend the rest of his life as a trapper of beaver and otter, to become one with the wilderness, as he phrased it. Nothing would please him more, he intoned solemnly, than to leave behind civilization's stinkpots, as he called the eastern cities. Though Annabelle had no difficulty understanding and even sharing his dislike for their grime and smoke and close confinement, she could not and did not encourage his wildly overstated, extreme sentiments.

An avid student of the French philosopher Rousseau, Balfour was certain that it was only the constricting confinements of human institutions, the unnatural and pernicious imprisonment of man's basically good and natural instincts, that had made man the unpalatable creature he was. Out here, he was sure, he would find man as he was meant to be, a noble creature of the forest, brother to the bird and the buffalo, kin to all living creatures. He was, he assured her quite seriously, returning to Eden.

Annabelle had listened patiently to these sentiments all during the voyage upriver and was painfully aware that Balfour knew nothing—absolutely nothing—about this land or the savages he would soon be living among. But she knew also that there was nothing she could tell him. He would have to grow up by himself in this cruel, inhospitable wilderness. If he survived, he would know then how utterly wrong he had been about practically everything. And if he did not survive, none of what he thought now would matter.

Pitying his ignorance, knowing the painful reality that lay before him, she forced herself to tolerate him and never ventured to disagree with him, while never mentioning her own tragic history among the Comanche and Comancheros. To him she was a refined woman from the perfumed society of Cambridge, and he took her silent acceptance of his long philosophical discourses and his foolish tirades against the civilization he had just left for agreement.

Now, pointing to the fort, Brad said, almost reverently, "There it sits, Mrs. Merriwether!"

"Yes, Brad. I see it."

"And look at all those Indian tents about it. There must be twenty or thirty. You know, Mrs. Merriwether, I think it is the most beautiful sight in the world."

She glanced at him in some surprise. His extravagant joy at sight of the fort astounded her. But she simply nodded and turned her attention back to the fort and said nothing to bring him back to reality.

She was too wrapped up in her own emotions anyway to bother with the young man's eager ramblings. A deep, abiding part of her had come home, and soon she would be with her brother again. She could almost sense his presence as he waited with the others for the steamboat to dock. Kenneth Mackenzie, the part-owner of the American Fur Company who managed this Upper Missouri Outfit, as it was called, would be waiting just as eagerly as the trappers and Indians for the precious goods stored in the hold below to be unloaded and brought into the fort for trading.

Already she could make out a colorful crowd growing along the shore and the heavy clot of men waiting on the landing. This appearance of the *Aissiniboin* as it steamed beyond the headlands and into the clear could not have been a surprise for any of them, she knew. The smoke from the steamboat's twin stacks lifting into the sky downstream must have been visible to watchers on the bluffs for a full day—perhaps even longer.

She began to make out the features on the faces of Indians and white men standing along the shore now, and she heard the captain order the gangplank to be untied. It was time for her to go to her room and get her things. She did not need to pack. Her steamer trunk had been packed for a full day now.

"I must leave you now, Brad," she told Balfour.

"Do you need help with your trunk?" he asked, turning almost regretfully from the railing.

"No, I'll be fine, Brad," she assured him.

She left him then and hurried off, her heart pounding in anticipation.

But as she stepped off the gangplank onto the landing, she saw no sign of Jed among the men pressing about the *Assiniboin*. She stood for a moment, looking beyond those just in front of her, but as the *engagés* crowded down the gangplank behind her, she was forced to move on farther down the landing. Smiling, courteous, even awed faces broke before her, and a moment later, still looking hopefully about her, it dawned on her that Jed was not going to show up. If he was at the fort, he would have been on that landing to greet her.

Brad Balfour materialized beside her. For a moment she was too astonished to greet him. On the voyage up the Missouri, he had dressed soberly enough in black pants, white broadcloth shirt, and a frock coat. But now he was wearing what he considered every well-dressed frontiersman wore: a fringed buckskin jacket and leggings, moccasins, and a coonskin cap, complete with tail. That he wasn't carrying a long Kentucky rifle was a blessing.

He saw the look on her face and mistook it for approval. Smiling proudly, he confided, "I been saving this outfit. I bought it in St. Louis."

"Is that so?"

"I got a long Kentucky rifle, too. But it's packed with all my other gear." He looked around, his eyes wide with excitement, then back at her. "Isn't your brother here, Mrs. Merriwether?"

"It doesn't look like it," she admitted.

"Where's your luggage?"

"I paid one of the French traders to bring it to the fort," she said.

"You didn't need to do that. I could have taken care of that for you."

"Thank you, Brad," she said, sighing. "Would you mind accompanying me to the fort?"

"I would deem it a privilege," he said with generous gallantry. "Indeed, it will make me the envy of every man on this post."

As Annabelle and Balfour trudged toward the fort, she saw a man she thought might well be Kenneth Mackenzie, two enormous wagons rumbling along beside him as he headed for the landing. For a moment she considered stopping him to ask about Jed—certain the American Fur Company official would know her brother by now. But she realized that this was not a good time to bother such a busy man.

Reaching the fort, they entered through the main gate, and at once Annabelle recognized a mountain man standing just inside the fort, a short, pudgy Indian woman at his side. Old Bill was, she remembered, a good friend of Jed's. Though she had met Old Bill only once in passing at Fort Hall, she would never have been able to forget his wild, ravaged figure. He was a little more than six feet in height, gaunt, red-haired, with a hard, weather-beaten face, marked deeply with smallpox.

Old Bill saw her, and his face lit in sudden recognition as he rushed over to her in that curious, staggering gait of his, leaving his Indian woman behind.

"You'd be Annabelle," he cried, in his curious, high-pitched voice. "Hawk's sister! Now what in tarnation're you doin' here? Thought you was living in the East, all married up good and proper."

"My husband is joining me soon, Bill. But I expected Jed to be waiting here. Have you seen him?"

"Last I knowed, he was off trappin' some beaver streams with an old Nez Percé chief."

"But I sent a letter to Fort Hall."

"When did you send it?"

"Nearly two months ago. You don't think Jed's been hurt, do you?"

"Hell's fire. Nothin' could hurt that feller. More'n likely your letter is still on the way to him. The last mail sack come from the East got here on a keel boat two weeks ago. If'n your letter was in there, it'll likely take a while to get to him. Thing is, Mackenzie ain't that all fired eager to send on any mail to a Hudson's Bay post."

"I should have realized," Annabelle sighed. "There are no post offices out here. This isn't Cambridge."

"Reckon that's a fact, Annabelle. My, you sure do look pretty."

"Thank you, Bill."

"And who might this pilgrim be?" Old Bill asked, peering with comical intensity at the buckskin-clad Balfour as he would at a strange and colorful bird strutting from behind a bush.

Annabelle hastily introduced Balfour to Bill, managing to slip in that the young man was intent on becoming a fur-trapper, like Bill.

"Are you, now?" Bill remarked, facing Balfour squarely and looking him up and down critically. "Well, now, Mr. Balfour, you'll need a sight more equipment than you got there—and that's a fact. Where'd you buy them fancy duds?"

"St. Louis."

"Thought so. Look store-bought. Won't last long here. You'll need to find yourself an Indian woman to make you proper buckskin leggings and a shirt— somethin' that won't turn to paper in the first rain."

"You mean I should marry an Indian squaw?"

"Didn't say marry and didn't say squaw. I said find an Indian woman to take care of you. Like my Mandan woman over there. She can sew up a storm, clean a buffalo skin, cook, hunt, find roots to cure what ails you. And she can make a man feel like a man when it comes time to blow out the candle."

"Well," Balfour stammered, glancing nervously at Annabelle, "I haven't thought that far ahead."

"You'd better. Pilgrim like you won't last a winter without a woman."

Balfour shifted uncomfortably. It was clear to Annabelle he was too embarrassed to discuss this topic in front of her. But to Annabelle, it was also clear Bill was talking good sense, though, of course, for her to admit this to Balfour would only embarrass the young man still further. Indeed, he would probably be shocked.

"If these clothes aren't suitable," Balfour told Bill hastily in an effort to change the subject, "I have additional clothing in my trunks. And I should be able to purchase any further items I might need at this fort. Don't you think?"

"Why, sure I think, sonny. I have to—all the time. Couldn't keep my topknot on if I didn't think. Now, you stay here with Annabelle and I'll go fetch Mac. He doesn't know Annabelle's here, and he'll sure want to meet her."

"Oh, now, don't bother him, Bill," Annabelle protested. "I'm sure he must be very busy."

"Won't be that busy," Bill assured her. "He'll be wanting to talk to Golden Hawk's sister, don't you worry none about that. Besides," he added, his eyes gleaming, "it might mean an invite for us to dine with him tonight. So you just stay put, Miss Annabelle, and I'll go get him."

As Balfour watched Old Bill hurry out through the gate, he frowned and looked with some concern back at Annabelle. "What a strange man! Does he ever wash?"

"Not if he can help it. Old Bill and water are not on speaking terms. But he's a good sort and a fine friend."

"Your friend?"

"Yes. Of me and of Jed, and of many other mountain men in this region."

"Why does he walk like that? It looks like he's drunk, but I don't think he is."

Annabelle shrugged. "I don't know. But no one pays any attention." She smiled. "From what I have heard, it doesn't prevent Old Fetchum from hitting what he aims at."

"Old Fetchum?"

"His rifle."

"Oh."

An awkward silence followed and Annabelle realized that Balfour was gathering the nerve to ask a personal question. She waited patiently and at last he cleared his throat. "Mrs. Merriwether . . . ?"

"What is it, Brad?"

"I think you've been holding out on me."

"Why, Brad, whatever do you mean?"

"You didn't tell me you knew this mountain man. I'll bet you know all these people. You've been out here before. But you just told me you were coming out here to visit your brother."

"I have not held out on you, Brad. I told you I was on my way to meet my brother. And that is the absolute truth. I also told you that my husband will join me as soon as he can, that he will be heading an expedition west to Oregon. What more do you have to know?"

He frowned. "Well, yes, I know . . . you did tell me that much. And I don't mean to pry. But just now I got the impression you haven't told me . . . well, a great deal, at least as much as you might have."

"Of course I haven't, Brad," Annabelle said with a smile. "That would take too long."

29

"It would?"

"And, besides," she said, laughing, "you and that philosopher, Jean-Jacques Rousseau, never gave me a chance to tell you much of anything."

Balfour looked more than a little flustered; then, to Annabelle's vast amusement, he blushed.

— 3 —

Kenneth Mackenzie, as Old Bill had surmised, did indeed invite Annabelle to his quarters that evening for dinner, quarters that Annabelle found surprisingly luxurious. She could tell that Brad Balfour was equally impressed. The apartment was spacious and well-furnished. The dining table was covered with fine damask and illuminated by buffalo tallow candles set in splendid silver candlesticks. There was a billiard table at one end of the big room before a huge fireplace, and a well-stocked bar. Chilled mint juleps were served in fine, narrow-stemmed glasses, and there was ice for the drinks from the icehouse Mackenzie had built near the river. The mint for their drinks came from the wild mint found in a spot more than a dozen miles away along the banks of the Yellow Stone River.

In addition to Old Bill, herself, and Brad, Mackenzie had invited to dinner the captain of the *Assiniboin* along with a French Canadian named Baptiste Lernier and another mountain man, Dick Wooton. Mackenzie was a tall, silver-haired man, whose soft voice and gentle bearing seemed surprising in a man directing the activities of a trading post so remotely situated and conducting at times such a bloody and dangerous trade. This was especially apparent to those around the table when he recalled his most recent difficulty in getting the Blackfoot Confederacy to allow him to build a fort farther up the Missouri in the middle of their hunting lands. The matter was still in some doubt, though he was hoping to build the fort next spring.

After the mint juleps, there was a feast of beef and venison and duck, during which the talk kept mainly to the troubling decline in the demand for beaver, which everyone blamed on the change in men's and women's fashion, which no longer seemed to demand beaver hats. Dick Wooton reminded everyone that it was probably a good thing, since prime beaver were getting scarce, anyway, and the best streams had been trapped out already.

Mackenzie predicted that soon buffalo hides would be worth as much or more than beaver. It was for this reason that he was encouraging the Blackfoot tribes to bring him all the buffalo hides they could, thereby undercutting the influence of the Hudson's Bay Company, with which the Blackfoot had long preferred to trade. The Hudson's Bay traders were unable to take buffalo pelts in any great amount since it was nearly impossible for them to ship them east on their canoes, while Mackenzie's steamboat could handle all the buffalo hides the Blackfoot could bring him.

"Don't you think the buffalo will soon be wiped out as a result?" asked Balfour. "Just as it seems the beaver are now dying out."

"The buffalo, sonny," drawled Old Bill, "cover these high plains like a blanket. And there's another herd, bigger than this one, farther on down that reaches clear into Texas."

Dick Wooten chuckled in agreement. "That's right, Balfour. You might as well talk about drawing the ocean dry."

After that, talk drifted to other things—such as which tribes were allied with which. There was much pondering and guessing about the relative strength and influence of certain warlike chiefs and their war parties. At the end of it, there was general agreement that if the Shoshone chief, Washoki, could keep his young bloods in control, it would be a relatively peaceful fall. There was, as usual, no fear of the Crows—not openly, at least; but there was always going to be difficulty with the Blackfoot tribes. Everyone conceded this, though there was some hope that eastern tribes like the Sioux, which were drifting into the plains, just might give the Blackfoot enough of a challenge to keep them busy.

As Annabelle listened, she concluded that nothing had changed during her years in the East. The various tribes were busy, as usual, killing and warring on each other without letup, like children playing in the back lot behind her house in Cambridge. Only they used real arrows and guns, and real women and children died with each village attacked, each glorious raid consummated.

Finally, as they left the table and moved farther down the huge room to the billiard table and the fireplace, Mackenzie came over to Annabelle and with a courteous bow gave her what he hoped would be good news, namely that he had spoken to a freighter, Cal Banyan, who was taking a caravan south to Fort Hall the day after tomorrow. The man had graciously consented to escort Annabelle to the fort.

". . .and I am reliably informed," Mackenzie continued, "that Jed has been seen in the vicinity of Fort

Hall throughout this past summer. In the accompany of an old Nez Percé chief, from what I hear."

Old Bill weaved over. "Just heard what you said, Mac. Thing is, I was plannin' on headin' south myself." He looked at Annabelle. "Hope you won't mind if I tag along, Annabelle."

Annabelle knew immediately why Bill was inviting himself, and she was grateful. They would be going through wild country, and his rifle would be most welcome.

"Of course not, Bill," she told him. "And I am sure Jed will be glad to see you."

"I'll be coming, too," Brad Balfour said, striding over. "Mr. Williams said he'd show me some fine beaver streams. And I want to make sure he does."

Bill winked at Annabelle. "I purely did say that, and I don't deny it." He turned to Balfour then. "And tomorrow we'll spend some time getting you ready for the wild. First thing we'll do is burn them fancy duds you bought in St. Louis."

Brad swallowed. "If you say so."

"I do. Yes, I do."

Annabelle wondered if there would be any way for Balfour to get Old Bill to burn his own incredibly dirty, greasy buckskins. And then, God be praised, take a bath. But one look at Balfour and she realized the young man wouldn't be able to get Bill to do anything that radical.

Or that painful.

Five days later, the freight wagons were laboring through a dangerous bog just beyond a shallow creek that emptied into the Yellow Stone. Five of the six wagons had already traversed the quicksand, and the final wagon was being pulled through. But by this time the ground had been worked into a treacherous quagmire and the wagon was getting nowhere.

Standing on a patch of high ground, Annabelle watched, her face shaded by her bonnet's hood. Cal Banyon and his six teamsters were doing what they could to drive the wagon through the bog. Like the other wagons it was hauled by a double mule team, but the struggling beasts were having no appreciable effect on the heavily laden wagon's progress. The men were also struggling fruitlessly as they tried to push the wagon through the bog. They had already laid a bed of boughs and brush over the ground to give purchase for the wheels; nevertheless, the wagon was noticeably sinking.

The reins were in the hands of one of the teamsters, a small but powerful *engagé* who was slapping the long leathers with great enthusiasm. But when he glanced back and saw the wheels sinking, he snatched up a long bullwhip and began cracking it over the mules' backs as the men bent their shoulders once more to the sides and back of the wagon and began to heave. The wheels began to turn, ever so slowly. The wagon inched forward. Annabelle held her breath. She knew the wagon had to keep going, however slowly, for the moment it stopped, the wheels would slice through the layers of brush and sink once more into the quicksand.

Despite the effort, the wagon halted and the wheels did begin to sink. There was howling and cursing, and Annabelle saw Cal Banyan leave off his direction from solid ground, pull off his moccasins, and wade barefoot through sand and water to throw his impressive weight against the nearest wheel. Annabelle did not know if it was his strength, or the power of his example, but the wagon began to move again. Soon it was gaining speed and a moment later its front wheels dug into solid ground and the wagon surged forward. A triumphant shout went up and one of the men sent his cap into the air.

The sun, a great, oversized ball of red, was sitting on the western horizon just above the mountain peaks. Soon it would be dark. Cal Banyan directed the wagons toward a narrow strip of cottonwoods farther down the stream, where they would make camp.

Trudging along behind the wagons, Annabelle was joined by Brad Balfour, who dismounted from his horse to walk beside her. He had pitched in with the teamsters in the effort to move the wagons through the shallows. His leather breeches were dark with mud clear to his thighs, and he was still blowing like a draft horse. He grinned happily at Annabelle, his smile as fresh as on the morning they set out from Fort Union, and proceeded to regale her with the many wonderful sights he had glimpsed during this day's journey.

Riding with Old Bill along the Yellow Stone River, he had witnessed great herds of buffalo swimming the river, so dense in spots that Old Bill had reckoned that Balfour could have walked across the river upon their great humped backs. He had spotted numberless elk and deer in the groves and slopes some distance from the river's bank, and over many of the open bottomlands he had glimpsed bands of antelope gliding swiftly, changing direction and speed with an effortlessness that was pure magic. In addition, he had sighted on nearly every butte and cliff looming above the river flocks of bighorn sheep.

As if this were not enough, a little after the noon stop, he had seen grizzly bears splashing about in the river's shallows, while packs of wolves and coyotes swept back and forth across the river and the bottoms, many feeding on the buffalo caught in the mud or on their great, swollen corpses putrefying along the banks or swept up onto the river's many sandbars.

All this, Brad recounted to Annabelle with an enthusiasm that did much to preclude her from joining in. All it remained for her to do was listen and nod. When Old Bill joined them, leading his horse, upon which his Mandan woman rode, he too found it impossible to get a word in edgewise. Glancing at Annabelle, he simply grinned and shrugged his shoulders before Balfour's eager torrent of observations.

Old Bill had done a fine job of outfitting Balfour in typical trapper's garb. Slung from Brad's saddle horn was a leather pouch holding six newly purchased beaver traps. Tied behind his saddle was a rolled blanket containing an extra pair of moccasins. From Balfour's belt hung his powder horn and bullet pouch in addition to a large, mean-looking butcher knife and a wooden box containing bait for beaver. On a leather thong about his neck hung a tobacco sack with a pipe and implements for making fire, and fastened to the pommel of his saddle was a sling containing a war hatchet.

Balfour's dress was in noticeable contrast to what he was wearing when he left the steamboat. His shirt was of antelope skin, which answered the purpose of both over and undershirt. He wore a pair of leather breeches with smoked buffalo skin leggings and a coat made from a red trade blanket, over which he had flung a long buffalo robe. His cap was of otter skin, and Balfour wore it at a suitably jaunty angle, so that it resembled somewhat the berets worn by the *engagés*. His feet were wrapped in strips of blanket, then cov-

ered with a pair of moccasins made of dressed deerskin. These, Annabelle knew, had been fashioned by
Buffalo Flower, Old Bill's Mandan woman, and were
a gift from her to Old Bill's new friend, as she referred
to Balfour. Though Brad did not have the long, greasy
hair hanging clear to his shoulders favored by most
mountain men, he nevertheless resembled a mountain
man as much as he could have wished at this stage,
and it was clear to Annabelle that he wore his new
outfit and brandished his gear with a great deal of
pride.

His rifle, which he had purchased in Ilion, New
York, was built by Eliphalet Remington. It was a
flintlock muzzle-loader, massive but beautiful in de-
sign and good in balance, as Balfour expressed it.
From all she could see, he was a fine marksman with
the rifle, and a few days before, he had earned a
begrudging mutter of approval from Old Bill when he
brought down a mule deer from a considerable distance without getting out of his saddle.

All that remained, it seemed to her, was for Balfour to
spend a long and bitter winter high in the mountains—or
find himself dealing with an angry war party of Blackfoot
or Comanches. This last she did not really wish on
him, however, and she chided herself for even contem-
plating it.

When they reached the cottonwoods, Balfour and
Old Bill left her to search for firewood, while she sat
under a tree and took off her bonnet, revealing her
golden hair, burnished like old brass, done up in pig-
tails and folded neatly across her head like a coronet.
She was wearing a long blue dress with cotton ruffles
at her wrists and neck, and on her feet high-laced,

leather boots. Despite the bonnet, her face had been bronzed by the sun, causing her light blue eyes to glow with an almost unearthly warmth.

When the men brought the firewood and dumped it at an appropriate spot for the night's campfire, she left the tree and busied herself building a fire, as had become her custom. One of the men rode up with a shoulder of elk, freshly killed, and reined in his horse to wait while a suitable spit was constructed. As Annabelle worked at her task, Buffalo Flower joined her, and for this Annabelle was grateful.

But not because she was lonely or needed the help.

Annabelle's problem was that she was finding it difficult to withstand alone the gaze of so many men. There was nothing malicious in their glances; the problem was that they were so grateful for the sight of a white woman that their intense gaze seemed almost to draw vitality from her. She knew that none of the men represented a threat to her. In fact, she knew there was not a man there who would not give his life, if need be, to keep her from harm. Yet, though this fact comforted her, it also unwittingly transformed her into a creature entirely too rare and too valued. She was, after all, just another traveler in a wild country.

What the West needed, she realized with a pang, was more white women. These wild, unwashed men needed their gentling influence even more than they needed soap and water.

That night came their first brush with Indians.

Banyan had circled the wagons and Annabelle was asleep in her sugan under one of them. So closely drawn together were the wagons that the forward wheel of one wagon nested close against the rear wheel of the wagon ahead. All the horses and mules had been turned loose into the corral formed by the ring. Brad Balfour was sleeping outside her wagon, a rear wheel separating him from Annabelle. Old Bill and Buffalo Flower, as was their custom, had made a separate camp some distance from the ring of wagons.

The startled whinny of a horse caused Annabelle to sit bolt upright, her head almost striking the wagon's undercarriage. From the other side of the corral came a sudden commotion. Shouts pierced the night. A flurry of hoofbeats drummed, a rifle cracked. Beyond the wagon wheel, Balfour flung off his blanket and rose to his feet, his Remington rifle already in hand. As Brad vanished toward the commotion, a cry swept about the wagons: "Indians!"

Annabelle heard someone galloping toward the wagons and then the sharp report of a rifle. An Indian cried out and Annabelle heard clearly the sound his body made as he thumped to the ground not ten feet from the wagon under which she now crouched, a long bowie knife in hand.

"Fort up!" Cal Banyan called. "Indians!"

This shout came from the other side of the wagons and she heard his horse as he galloped around the ring, arousing his teamsters. At the same time Annabelle thought she heard a more distant, barely audible thunder of hoofbeats. Could this mean still more Indians? Then, from the darkness south of them, came the distant rattle of rifle fire. Almost at once, it seemed, there was a sudden decrease of activity inside the corral. There were a few yelping, startled cries, and then the sound of unshod ponies heading north, pounding through the night, the noise of their flight rapidly diminshing.

Then silence.

Except for the growing thunder of pounding hooves coming from the other direction.

"Listen," called a hushed Balfour, crouched somewhere in the darkness just beyond Annabelle's wagon.

"Another war party," someone muttered nervously.

Banyan pulled up within a few feet of Annabelle's wagon. She peered up at him and saw the man peering into the night, his gaunt face intent. His horse shook its head, its bit jingling.

"No," Banyan said sharply, "it's white men! Hunters, maybe."

Then, out of the black night, high and clear above the pounding of the approaching hooves, came the call of a white man.

"Hello, the wagons!"

Annabelle almost leapt out from under the wagon. Outside the ring, she ran toward the horsemen galloping across the flat out of the night. Again came the hail to the wagons from the approaching rider.

Annabelle pulled up.

"Jed!" she called.

"Annabelle!"

Jed flung himself from his horse and for a wonderful, thrilling moment stood before her. Then he caught her up in a powerful bear hug. Out of pure relief and happiness, she felt tears coursing down her cheeks. For a few heart-stopping moments under that wagon, Annabelle had been certain she would never see Jed again. Terrible memories she had thought long dead had arisen from deep within her, threatening to overwhelm her.

But now those memories were gone; the strong arms of her brother had banished them completely.

— 4 —

A week later they arrived at Fort Hall, Old Bill making it a real occasion as he and the four mountain men who had accompanied Hawk discharged their rifles within sight of the fort, then booted their horses on ahead, unwilling to be kept back by the lumbering wagons.

A half-hour or so later Hawk and Annabelle, Brad Balfour alongside them, rode up to the fort's gate. They were a quarter of a mile or so ahead of the wagons. Standing just inside the gate beside his saddled horse, Annabelle saw the fort's chief factor hold up his hand in greeting. The three dismounted.

Introducing himself as Hamilton Walsh, the chief factor greeted Annabelle graciously, assuring her that he had readied an apartment for her and had instructed Joe Meek to take her to it. Then, excusing himself, the factor mounted up and rode out of the fort with four other employees of the Hudson's Bay Company to greet the incoming wagons.

Annabelle saw an old Nez Percé Indian also standing just inside the gate, and when Hawk espied him, he pulled Annabelle and Brad eagerly over to him and introduced them. The Nez Percé, whose name was Tames Horses, nodded to Annabelle, a pleased glint in his black eyes, then bid farewell to Jed in his own tongue. Mounting a beautiful Appaloosa, he rode out of the gate, leading a single packhorse. He waved once to Hawk and vanished from sight.

"Damn," said Jed with feeling. "I'll miss that man."

"I liked him," Annabelle said, and meant it.

"How old is he?" Balfour asked.

Jed shrugged. "I don't know. He's seen a few winters, though." Then Jed looked at Annabelle. "Let's go find Joe Meek. He must be around here somewhere."

As they proceeded into the inner court, Annabelle noticed how crowded it was with animals and people. She kept close to Hawk, remarking on the number of Indians. They were Crows mostly, but there were also a few Blackfoot, if she was not mistaken. Mountain men were everywhere, but more remarkable were the travelers dressed in eastern finery. Built along the log palisades on both sides of the courtyard, she saw, were rooms and quarters, rising two stories high and fronted by roofed verandas and balconies supported by sturdy beams.

"My," said Annabelle, "things look so different."

"This is Hudson's Bay's last stand, I'm thinking," Hawk told her. "And Walsh is determined not to let anyone drive him out. He might make it."

"You've been here before, too?" Balfour asked Annabelle.

"Yes, Brad," Annabelle told him, laughing.

"I give up," Balfour said, shaking his head in frustration. "Next thing, you'll be telling me you used to live out here—on a farm, or something."

Annabelle looked shrewdly at Brad for a moment,

considering whether or not to tell him all about it, then—after a quick glance from Jed—decided against it and said nothing.

Looking back around her as they crossed the courtyard, she realized suddenly that everyone was staring at her. Grizzled trappers and hunters gaped from their hairy, matted faces. The Indians pointed and stared, some even following after her. It was worse than it had been with the freighters.

But she understood. She was young, slender, lovely as a picture, and her face, she knew, was flushed with nervous excitement. She was wearing only a simple muslin dress and a plain straw bonnet trimmed with blue ribbon, the ribbon calculated to match her eyes. She saw the awe, even excitement, in the faces of the men watching her, and she realized how much her full skirt emphasized her narrow waist, and her shaped bodice the full roundness of her bosom.

It was no wonder that on this distant outpost so far from civilization she would be the sole object of every male pair of eyes as she accompanied her brother across the courtyard, and what she felt was guilt that she had so aroused these men, even though it had been entirely involuntary on her part.

Then, as Joe Meek appeared out of the crowd and hurried toward them, she saw a pair of eyes looking at her with such a feral intensity that her skin crawled.

"Jed," she whispered urgently, her fingers tightening about his arm, "that man over there—the one on the balcony—who is he?"

"A mountain man who got chewed up some by a grizzly," he told her. "Tames Horses and I helped him to

Fort Hall about two weeks ago. He was in bad shape then, but it looks like he's up and about."

Almost furtively Annabelle studied the man. He was a great, hulking six-footer, wearing dirty buckskins fringed so copiously he seemed to be dripping dirty strings of leather. He was as broad and thick as a good-sized oak. His matted beard and skin were the color of old bark. And the brightness in his blue eyes and the intensity of his stare sent a cold shudder through her, and she looked quickly away.

Joe Meek caught Annabelle's reaction immediately. Stepping along beside her, he leaned his head closer and said, "Don't let that man bother you now. And if he comes near you, just let out a howl. Hawk brought him in and he can send him packin' just as easy."

"There's no need for that, Joe," Annabelle protested. "He's done me no harm. It's just that he has such a . . .wild look."

"And a wild heart, I'm thinkin'," said Joe Meek. "I been watching that one these past two weeks. He stays by hisself, like a hurt dog. Man like that, he goes his own way. Old Bill knows him some, but ain't nobody else knows a thing about him—where he's been, where he's goin'—and there ain't a one of us knows what's in that heart of his."

Hawk laughed. "You make him sound like a bogeyman, Joe. You trying to scare Annabelle?"

"Ain't nothin' goin' to scare this woman," Joe Meek said, gazing fondly at Annabelle.

Annabelle blushed. And, deep inside, wished it were true. "Thanks, Joe. You make me feel ten feet tall."

With Joe Meek in the lead, they all trooped up the rough wooden steps leading to the second-floor balcony.

*   *   *

As Gar Trimm descended the stairs farther down the wall and headed for the grog shop near the stables, he carried before him a picture of Annabelle as clearly as if he were looking into a painting—a painting that moved and lived, that was achingly, beautifully alive. He did not have to make any effort to recall the blond woman's features. They appeared before his mind's eye unbidden, without conscious volition.

Only once before had he seen a woman as beautiful as Annabelle—many, many years ago, when he was not yet five and his mother had leaned close to him while he lay in his perambulator. She had kissed him lightly on the cheek, tucked the warm blankets around him— and then, laughing gaily, had set off, pushing the baby carriage over rough sidewalks, the noisy swarm of traffic enclosing him. What followed then was monumental, terrifying confusion: screams, the rattle of wagons, and the shrill whinnying of horses. In a bewildering succession a storm of faces peered down at him. He heard sharp cries, voices harsh and unkind, and then felt rough, uncaring hands pluck him from his blanket.

He never saw his mother again, only pale, weeping faces framed in black veils and wide-brimmed hats; and with his mother gone—and what had happened to her he gradually realized he would never know—his father found him too awkward and demanding to care for and sent him to live with a gray haired old crone who beat him as easily and as casually as she lifted beer to her lips.

In the nightmare years that followed he searched everywhere for his mother's face. At night he lay awake aching for the love and warmth that he had last know when his mother leaned close and kissed him.

But her face never materialized out of any crowd, and the ache in his heart descended into the deepest seams of his being, like a kind of rheumatism of the soul, leaving him with a deep, scouring sense of loss that never completely vanished.

Growing up with the old crone in a dank, windowless world of lice-infested beds and foul-smelling slops jars, padding on bare feet over floors carpeted by scurrying cockroaches, fed only white tea and barely palatable crusts of bread, he rose up at last after a particularly merciless beating, snatched the broom handle from the old woman, and in a revolution that cheered his soul, beat the harridan to within an inch of her life and fled forever her pestilential prison.

Sleeping afterward at odd hours under steps and in back alleys, a filthy, unkempt boy running as wild as any fabled youngster suckled by wolves, he became by the age of thirteen a streetwise street urchin, a thief when opportunity beckoned, and a snarling, slashing cur when apprehended. By the time he was sixteen years of age his appetites were as untamed as his behavior, and he was as wild and as dangerous as any of the pigs or wild dogs that roamed at will through the manure-laden streets and back alleys of St. Louis.

Finally, in flight from what little law there was in that city, he stowed away on one of the flatbed keelboats heading up the Missouri River on a trapping expedition led by General William Ashley. Eighteen years old now, as strong as a young ox, and already tall for his age, he was put to work with the French *engagés* to help in poling and cordelling the keelboat upriver, tasks for which his young, stallion-like strength were ideally suited.

Soon after arriving in the wilderness, he learned his

trade as a fur-trapper, and after Ashley was bought out by the American Fur Company, he left the four companions he had been trapping with and set out on his own. In the years since, he had become more and more of a loner, trapping by himself, retreating deeper and deeper into the high Rockies. He sought out the lush, hidden valleys threaded by slow streams and lost lakes, until he found at last the valley that became for him a fortress of isolation as well as a bountiful source of beaver plews and wild game.

Peering through the grog shop's open doorway, Gar saw Old Bill Williams sitting at a table in a corner. He knew Bill to be a loner, like himself, only like Gar he needed a woman to cook for him and keep his lodge clean. No longer living with the Ute, he traveled with a Mandan woman and did not seem inclined to shuck her off.

As Gar pushed into the low-ceilinged, smoky interior of the place, Bill caught sight of him and raised his whiskey glass in salute. Gar took it for an invitation to join him at his table.

Gar pushed through the crowd of men, sat down across from Bill, and beckoned to the bartender, who hurried over with a glass and a bottle.

Bill spun a coin onto the table. "Leave the bottle, hoss," he told the bartender in his high, squeaky voice. "This child'll be needin' it. I been eating dust all the way from Fort Union."

The aproned fellow slapped the bottle down on the table between the two mountain men, scooped up the coin, and vanished into the smoke. Old Bill poured, then pushed the bottle toward Gar.

"You look sour, Gar, but then, you never could find a reason for a smile."

Gar poured his drink, drank it down, and let the fiery liquor warm his gullet, then spread itself through his vitals, thinking with renewed resentment of how poorly he had done when he became well enough to trade his plews.

To his astonishment he had been offered even less than what they had brought the year before—only a dollar a plew for skins averaging one and a half pounds. If that were not enough, the trader had added insult to injury by offering only half-price for those plews that bore talon marks, no matter how slight and inconsequential they were. Though Gar had stalked out in anger at this, in the end he had been forced to capitulate. In all, his entire winter take—less those that had been damaged beyond redemption by the grizzly—had netted him only two hundred dollars.

"What's goin' on, Bill?" Gar demanded sullenly. "Beaver ain't bringin' what it used to."

"Beaver's done, Gar. Ain't you heard?"

"How could that be?"

"Ain't usin' 'em for hats no more."

"Why not?"

"Fashion, Gar. It's what we's all slaves to."

"Don't know what the hell yer talkin' about, Bill."

"Didn't figure you would. But the truth of it is there's nary a place left for varmints like you and me. Them's gone under, what we shed tears for. They's fortunate they didn't hold up for such times as these." His bright eyes regarded Gar narrowly, then glanced away. "Yessiree, you'd best do like me, and hire on to shoot meat for the greenhorns. It's all that's left."

Gar grunted and shook his head. Maybe for Bill, it was—but he still had his valley, a place like none other, and his own for as long as he could hold it.

"I'll be pullin' out soon, Bill. Ain't goin' to wet-nurse these here traders."

"You got a place, have you?"

Gar nodded.

"Plenty of beaver?"

"Game, too."

"What's keepin' you, then?"

"I lost my woman."

"What about mine?"

"She's too fat, Bill. And she's a Mandan."

"Good cook, Gar. And a comfort on the pine boughs."

Gar shook his head. He had seen Old Bill's woman when she rode in behind him earlier. He did not want her.

What he did want, he realized, was that woman with the golden hair, Hawk's sister. She stirred parts of him alive that had long seemed dead within him, like poking a stick through the ashes of a campfire. But of course she was out of the question for a man such as he. The startled, frightened look in her eyes when she caught his gaze had not gone unnoticed by him. He understood perfectly how she felt. What it all meant, he reckoned, was that from now on it would be difficult for him to be satisfied with an Indian woman.

A few days before, he had moved in with a Crow squaw and had found her lazy and independent, with a voice that set his teeth on edge. She had been spoiled rotten from dealing with the white men at the fort. Her greased hair crawled with graybacks, and the scraps that came out of her cooking pot were so bad Gar had spat them out onto the floor of her lodge in undisguised contempt for her abilities as a cook. He had already hauled his gear out of her tepee and was sleeping now in a stall at the rear of the fort.

"You goin' back south to Ute country?" Gar asked, pouring himself a second drink.

"I'd like to do that. Yes, I would. But I just heard. Them damn Utes is makin' trouble. Burning settlers' cabins, takin' white scalps. And this child's too long in the tooth to go on the warpath."

Gar nodded, finished his drink, and got up. He was too ignorant of society's graces to thank Bill for the drinks or bid him good-bye as he pushed through the smoke-laden air and left the place.

One of the Blackfoot Annabelle had noticed when she first entered the fort was named Two Bears, and he had noticed her as well. Golden Hawk he had also noticed, and when darkness fell, he slipped from the fort and galloped for close to a mile, coming to a halt at last in a small, stream-fed clearing, where he dismounted beside the glowing remnants of a campfire.

From the surrounding timber three Comanche warriors strode, leading their ponies. They greeted Two Bears with a simple, palm-up salute. They were Hears-the-Wind, Sky Pony, and Owl's Heart. Hears-the-Wind was a squat, bowlegged warrior; Sky Pony was a lean warrior with a straight brow and black eyes that glowed with a fierce light. The third Comanche was the shortest of the three, but the solid breadth of his shoulders more than compensated for his lack of height.

None of them had ever seen Golden Hawk, but Two Bears knew him by sight, and as he had promised, he had come out here to lead them to the enemy of both their people. On the ground beside the campfire's embers, the Blackfoot drew a plan of the fort.

Squatting about it, the four Indians conversed entirely in sign language, the universal language of the Plains Indians.

When Two Bears revealed that not only Golden Hawk but his sister, Sky Woman, was at the fort, the three Comanche could hardly contain their eagerness. Sky Pony was in charge of this raiding party, so it was he who led the silent, intent discussion, his hands writing swiftly in the air as he brought them around in quick, graceful motions, sometimes jabbing with the speed of a striking snake and occasionally punctuating his message with soft, guttural grunts.

Having spent much time with the white eyes as a trapper, Sky Pony was familiar with their forts and buildings. Indeed, his few detractors in the Kwahadi band said he sometimes smelled like a white man. Yet it was this knowledge of the white eyes that made Sky Pony's medicine powerful enough to lead this war party. For in the days of his wandering as a trapper, he had come upon Fort Hall and learned that Golden Hawk often brought his beaver plews to this fort. Sky Pony had returned then to his Kwahadi band and proposed his plan for this raid.

Now the time had come, and Sky Pony was eager to move out. He stood up and issued his orders, then swung onto his pony, the other two Comanche and Two Bears following suit. As they rode off, the moon's bright, gleaming disk was only slightly obscured by scudding clouds. They would have plenty of light for this night's raid.

— 5 —

Old Bill was drunk. Very drunk. Hawk looked down at him slumped over his table, and then at Joe Meek. Joe grinned and shrugged. The grog shop was empty of patrons now, except for Old Bill, but the smoke was still so dense Hawk's eyes were smarting.

"You take Bill's feet," Hawk told Joe, as he took Old Bill by the hair and pulled his head up off the table, the back of Bill's head catching the chair sharply, "and I'll take him under his shoulders."

Bill was a tall man and, despite his lanky appearance, as solid as mahogany. Lifting him out of his chair was not easy. The barkeep held the door open for them and they hauled Old Bill out into the courtyard. They were staggering slightly by the time they left the fort and came to a halt in front of Buffalo Flower's lodge. Without a word or greeting of any kind, she stepped out of the tepee and held the flap open for them. They deposited Old Bill on his couch and left him to Buffalo Flower.

Outside the fort Hawk and Joe paused for a breather, sitting down in the cool darkness, their backs against the palisades. The smell of Indian came from all around,

Indian ponies, especially. As Hawk took out his pipe and lit it, he glanced about him at the lodges, conical towers looming black against the moonlit sky.

He looked up at the moon as he puffed. The clouds passing before it were too insubstantial to do more than clothe it for a few moments at a time in a glowing, diaphanous scarf. He heard movement from a Crow lodge about a hundred yards away and saw a brave stand free of it and, like Hawk and Joe Meek, glance up at the moon.

"Annabelle looks mighty purty," Joe commented, sending smoke out through his nostrils. "That captain of hers is a lucky man."

"Annabelle wants me to join his expedition."

"Expedition?"

"The government's looking for an easy way to Oregon."

Joe Meek snorted. "That's what I been lookin' for close on to fifteen years."

"Well, Jim Merriwether's leading an expedition to find it, funded by the U.S. Congress and the Interior Department."

"And that's why Annabelle is out here?"

"That's one of her reasons."

"And the other's to see you, I'm thinkin'."

"I figured that, and maybe she's homesick. Strange as that may sound."

"It sure does sound strange, Hawk. After what she's been through in these parts."

"She told me she wants to go with Jim on the expedition. Says she could act as an interpreter. And maybe she could, at that."

"What do you think of the idea?"

"Don't much like it. She'd be a whole lot safer in

this fort. And I'll make that point to her husband when I see him."

"When's he due here?"

"In a month, maybe sooner. It's too late to take the steamboat. They plan on making straight for the pass overland, then swinging north up the Snake."

Puffing contentedly on his pipe, Joe said, "What about this here greenhorn's attached himself to Annabelle? Balfour. He's up there on the balcony with her now, I'll bet. He buzzes around her like a bee around honey. Not that I blame him."

"Puppy love, I call it. He's harmless, and Annabelle's glad for his company, I'm sure. Bill told me he's a good shot with that Remington."

"Hawk, that young man is so full of bullshit he could spit and fertilize this side of the Rockies."

Hawk chuckled. "He's just read too many books, looks like. I'll let Old Bill handle him. He's read a few books himself, I hear."

"I hear tell he translated the Bible into Osage." Joe Meek chuckled and glanced in the direction of Buffalo Flower's lodge. "But I don't guess it done him or them Osage much good."

The smell of Indian became suddenly overpowering and it wasn't a horse. A twig snapped behind Hawk. He heard Joe Meek's sudden intake of breath and then his curse. Hawk was leaping to his feet and turning when the palisade wall crashed down onto his skull. As he crumpled into darkness, he felt a blade slice into his back, deep. . . .

A moment before, Sky Pony had held up his hand to stop Owl's Heart and Hears-the-Wind. Two Bears had already left them. The two white men smoking their pipes before the gate were directly in their path and would have to be struck down—quickly and silently.

Sky Pony glanced quickly at Owl's Heart and pointed to the small, round-faced one. Owl's Heart nodded and stepped quickly up behind the small man and raised his war club. Lifting his own club, Sky Pony took out his knife and stepped up behind the other one. His foot came down on a twig, snapping it. As Owl's Heart brought his war club down on the smaller one, the other white man, alerted by the snapped twig, leapt to his feet and started to turn.

Before the white man could turn completely, Sky Pony clubbed him viciously to the ground, then plunged his knife into the man's back. As Sky Pony pulled his knife out, he debated whether or not to take the white man's scalp but he had crushed the white man's broad-brimmed hat down over his head, and there was no time to lift it off and take his trophy. Wiping his blade off on his thigh, Sky Pony stepped over the man he had just killed, skirted around the crumpled figure of the other one, and with his two companions in single file behind him, slipped into the fort and glanced quickly around.

Sky Pony's heart leapt in triumph. Two Bears' map of the fort had been so accurate he knew at once where he was. Searching to his right, he saw the balcony and the wooden stairway leading up onto it.

Keeping in the shadows, the three warriors trotted along the wall until they came to the stairway, then glided up to the balcony. Sky Pony paused. According to Two Bears' map, the lodge where Hawk and his sister were staying was only two doors down. Reaching it, he touched the knob, turned it, and pushed it open.

The white man's lodge was empty. Just inside the doorway, the three warriors stood, irresolute. Then Sky Pony heard voices and the sound of footsteps on the catwalk that ran along the top of the palisades. He led the others from the room, pulled the door shut, and slipped silently down the balcony.

Ahead of him on the catwalk Sky Woman and Golden Hawk were talking softly. Golden Hawk was wearing an otter-skin cap over his surprisingly short yellow hair. Sky Woman, wearing a long blue white woman's dress, had combed out her hair so that it flowed in a solid wave of shimmering gold down over her shoulders. Moving as silently as the moon flitting through the clouds above them, Sky Pony led his two companions onto the catwalk.

"But if you asked your brother," Brad pleaded, "I'm sure he'd recommend me to your husband."

"I don't think you're ready for such an expedition, Brad," Annabelle told him bluntly.

"Not ready?"

"You heard me."

"You mean I haven't killed any grizzly bears."

"I don't mean that at all, Brad. This will be a dangerous, grueling journey. Just stick with Old Bill. He'll teach you what you need to know."

"He's a drunk. Right now he's so soused, your brother's gone down to put him to bed. And if you've noticed, he's still not back yet."

"Maybe so, Brad, but Bill Williams is already a legend in these parts."

"A legend? You must mean his capacity for liquor."

Annabelle sighed. "I'm tired, Brad. Wait until James gets here. Let him decide. Meanwhile, why not help

Bill hunt fresh game for the fort? Mr. Walsh says they can use all the game you can bring down. It'll give you plenty of opportunity to practice with that fine new rifle of yours."

Brad sighed and looked out across the moonlit flat, somewhat mollified. He knew that Annabelle was right. Considering what she had been through, she certainly had to know what she was talking about. This evening, Balfour had learned some astonishing things about Annabelle, and from her own lips. Most of what she had told him was pretty difficult to believe, but he believed her all right. Kidnapped and brought up by the Comanches, then sold to the Comancheros, married finally to a Shoshone warrior, and at the end of it all, losing her infant son to an attacking Crow war party.

What really amazed him was that Annabelle had returned voluntarily to what she herself called a murderous land.

He heard her gasp and turned his head to see a tall, granite-faced Indian clasping his hand about Annabelle's mouth. Before he could react, his own arms were pinned behind him as a third pair of hands closed tightly about his mouth to prevent an outcry. He struggled futilely and for a moment was able to pull his face away from the sweaty hands over his mouth. But even as he pulled away a piece of rawhide was thrust into his mouth, and a moment later, a crushing blow on the top of his head turned his knees to water.

Watching from the shadows in front of the stable, Gar Trimm was silent as he followed the three Comanches from the fort and saw them mount up and ride off with the girl and her brother. He saw which direction they took, and as their unshod hoofbeats faded, he returned to the fort for his saddle horse and pack mule.

He was in no hurry. He would make his move all in good time. He didn't much care what happened to Golden Hawk. It was Hawk's golden-haired sister he cared about. After them three Comanche got through with her, she would be pared down to his size for sure.

As he rode out through the fort's gate, this mean thought caused him to chuckle with cold appreciation.

The two bodies that lay crumpled in the high grass beside the fort's wall attracted little attention. In the first gray light of dawn, a few dogs sniffed first at Hawk's body, then Joe Meek's, after which, tails drooping, they trotted off, following other scents. The many Indian women gathering firewood in the timber behind the fort were too heavily laden to change direction when they glimpsed the two white men asleep on the ground, and made no effort to inspect them.

It was, after all, something the Indian women had come to expect. Their own men would drink to a kind of fatal oblivion and remain unconscious for hours wherever they collapsed, many times not returning to their fogged, ugly senses until well past midday. It was not unusual behavior for them, and to a somewhat lesser extent, for the hunters, mountain men, and employees of the fort. It was clear to the Indian women and the old men wrapped in blankets who came out to wash in the stream beside the fort, that the two men in the deep grass were simply sleeping off the effects of the whiskey they had consumed the night before.

As a result, the Indians were careful not to disturb

them. There was nothing more touchy or mean than a man awakening from a drunken stupor, his clothes reeking of stale vomit and piss, his breath like that of a toothless bear, and his head rocking in agony. It was always best to give such victims of their own thirst a wide berth.

Inside the fort, business proceeded as usual. Cal Banyan was busy loading his wagons, and this was not easy, since so many of his teamsters were feeling the effects of last night's carousal, and many of his mules had to be shod or replaced.

Hamilton Walsh was still busy overseeing the storage of the goods brought in by Banyan and compiling a list of goods he wanted Cal to bring on his next trip. That Annabelle Merriwether had not shown up for the morning breakfast caused him to wonder slightly, but he had no doubts about her safety with Golden Hawk at her side. He'd heard from the grog shop's owner that Hawk and Joe Meek had carried Old Bill out a little before midnight, soused to the gills, and the stable hostler reported that sometime during the night Gar Trimm had pulled out.

That Gar had done so in the middle of the night worried Walsh only a little. He was glad to be rid of Gar. The trapper's calmest remark resembled at best the snarl of an irritated bear. He was an unpleasant creature of the wild, with none of the graces of a civilized man, and Walsh hoped they'd seen the last of him for a while. It was Old Bill Williams, weaving precariously toward the fort, who rescued the two bodies outside the gate. Pulling up and squinting carefully at them, he recognized Hawk's wide-brimmed hat and then caught the spill of his long golden hair.

His crooked gait took him to the two men's side in a

rush, and dropping beside Hawk, he saw the knife wound. As he pushed him forward to examine the wound more closely Hawk's hat rolled off his head and Old Bill saw the skull laceration, noting the hardening cap of coagulating blood that darkened Hawk's hair. There were so many flies crawling over the bloody scab, it appeared to have a life of its own.

Joe Meek had not been stabbed, and when Old Bill flung him over onto his back, the tough little man blinked his eyes painfully, tried to sit up, and then collapsed back down into the grass. Despite everything Old Bill could do after that, Joe remained unconscious.

Old Bill hurried into the fort to raise the alarm, and soon found out the worst, that Annabelle and the tenderfoot Balfour had been taken, by whom, no one had the slightest idea.

There were two doctors in the fort. Phineas P. Burke, M.D., was a frock-coated dandy who had purchased his medicine and black leather bag from a mail-order firm located in Philadelphia; the other was Terence Wheelock, a veterinarian whom Hamilton Walsh employed to look after his stock. He was gentle with the animals and on more than one occasion had saved a horse or mule from execution by his uncanny ability to set bones. As a result, Walsh had come to rely on Wheelock for human ailments as well, finding him an excellent diagnostician with a wide variety of natural cures in his pharmacopoeia.

But it was Phineas P. Burke who first looked after Hawk and the first thing Burke did was bleed him, ostensibly to enable Hawk to regain consciousness. It did nothing of the sort and when Hawk did come to his senses, he was as weak as a kitten. Meanwhile, the doctor, concentrating entirely on Hawk's knife wound, entirely missed the concussion Hawk had sustained, despite Hawk's near inability to talk coherently.

When Walsh saw this, he dismissed Burke out of hand and brought in the veterinarian, who stopped bleeding Hawk and kept him still until the effects of the concussion had worn off. Joe Meek had only a sore head and had not lost any blood, so he was up and about long before Hawk.

Three days after being struck down, Hawk and Joe took after the Comanche raiding party.

Following the abduction, the three Comanche rode with their two captives through the entire day, pausing only for water. At dusk, they entered a secluded ravine and made camp beside a stream. Until now they had seemed tireless, indifferent to the bone-jarring miles.

Tied to her pony with rawhide attached to her ankles and passed under the pony's belly, Annabelle was exhausted, her thighs chafed raw by the rough blanket that served as a saddle.

It was the Comanche she had heard addressed as Sky Pony who untied her. Wearily, painfully, Annabelle slipped off the horse. She was in a furious daze at her sudden capture, incredulous that she had allowed this to happen. But over it all hung a bitter resignation. After all, she asked herself bitterly, what had she expected would happen when she returned to this savage land? She had allowed her distance from it over the past years to cloud her awareness of its terrible reality, to blur its sharp, cruel edges.

Looking now into the face of Sky Pony, she realized that those cruel edges were still there, as was the

Indian's naked, unashamed savagery. From the way Sky Pony spoke and from the attitude of the other two Indians toward him, she knew he was this raiding party's leader. He reached for her arm to help her steady herself. She pulled back, doing nothing to repress her loathing of him. His eyes lit briefly with a cold flare of emotion. He turned and stalked away, angry.

Watching him move off, Annabelle felt pure satisfaction. She stepped back from the pony and was turning when one of the other two Comanche grabbed her roughly and hauled her over to a spot under a tree, flinging her down beside Balfour, who had been dumped under it, his wrists still bound with rawhide. Because he had fought bitterly from the moment of his capture, the Comanche had beaten his face almost raw, and judging from the way he kept his left arm close against his chest, one of his ribs had probably been broken as well.

"Are you all right?" Brad managed as he turned to look at her.

Considering his own awful state, it was a question that revealed a deep, heartfelt concern for her, and Annabelle was deeply touched. "I'm all right, Brad. But you don't look so good."

"I think one of my ribs is broken."

"Don't struggle."

"You mean just let this happen?"

"They'll kill you."

"I can't understand why they haven't already."

"I think I know why."

"Tell me, then."

"They think you are Jed."

"You mean this is all a case of mistaken identity?"

"Jed has your height and build. And like you, he has blond hair."

"Annabelle, what is this all about?"

"I've told you about Jed and I being brought up by these Comanches. What I didn't tell you was that when Jed broke free of them, he killed one of their war chiefs and other warriors. Since that time, it has been a sort of ritual for any young Comanche to prove his manhood by coming after Jed."

"My God!"

"So far, Jed has eluded their young warriors. Not a single one who has come after him has returned. But this has only made the attempt to capture or bring back Jed's scalp all the more attractive."

"And now they think they have succeeded in capturing Jed."

"And his sister as well. These three Comanche are certain they will be very famous when they return with us to their village."

"But Jed will be after us."

"Yes," she replied, remembering then all the many nights when she had lain awake in Indian lodges dreaming of his arrival, of his swift and terrible justice when the time came. Even when it had seemed he would never find her, a small, tough part of her refused to give up hope. And then he had come for her, just as he had promised.

She saw Brad looking hopefully around him, as if he expected to see Jed step from the brush any minute, his rifle held ready. Annabelle sighed wearily. It would take time, she realized, for Jed to overtake these Comanche—and much could happen in the meantime.

"As long as they have us," she told Brad, "they won't be thinking Jed is on their trail."

"But what if they find out the truth—that I'm not Jed."

"They won't—not unless I tell them."

"Why would you do that?"

"Because you they might let live. Whereas Jed they will be eager to kill as soon as they get him back to their village."

"Kill him?"

"Of course. And slowly. Why do you suppose they have come this far to capture him?"

"My God! These Indians are barbaric! It's like some hideous nightmare."

"And the nightmare has just begun, Brad. I once called this a dark land. Now you see why. Your noble 'children of the forest,' as you once described them to me, are, in reality, killers and abductors who play games of war for want of something better to do. This is what your wilderness paradise produces without your irksome civilized restraints."

Balfour groaned. "My God. How could I have been so wrong?"

"It's called theory without the benefit of practice, I believe."

Glumly, Brad nodded, and when Annabelle saw his downcast look, it struck her as so comical that, despite their predicament, she laughed.

She would not laugh again for a long, long time.

In dealing with their enemies, the Blackfoot were a treacherous people. Two Bears was no exception and regarded the Comanche war party below him in the ravine as much an enemy of his people as the Crow, the Shoshone and the Nez Percé— all those tribes, in short, who were not of the Blackfoot Confederacy. That the three Comanche regarded Two Bears as an ally in their continuing struggle with the hated Golden Hawk filled Two Bears with a fierce, savage amusement. These three Comanche were regarded by him as beneath his contempt.

Two Bears had been perfectly willing to let Sky Pony enter Fort Hall and carry off Golden Hawk and his sister. That Sky Pony was such a fool as to have mistaken the pale easterner with the short-cropped golden hair as Golden Hawk only confirmed him in his estimation of Sky Pony's abilities. The Commanche had succeeded, however, in taking Golden Hawk's sister for there was no doubt in his mind that this was indeed Sky Woman, she who had borne the Shoshone warrior Crow Wing a son.

Sky Woman would make a fine addition to his household, but more important she would draw into Two Bears' web the real Golden Hawk.

And Two Bears had made his plans accordingly.

Now, below him in the ravine, as the Comanche were busy making camp, Hawk's sister was sprawled on the ground beside the eastern white man. It was time. Two Bears waved to his two companions on each side of him and at the third Blackfoot warrior crouched on the ravine's far bank. Then he stood up, uttered his fiercest war cry and let fly his first arrow.

The arrow's flight was true, catching the one called Hears-the-Wind in the chest. The Indian toppled backward into the fire as Two Bears' comrades sent their own arrows after his.

Though Sky Pony was caught in the thigh, he managed to snatch up his rifle and hatchet, then scramble up a slope and vanish. The third Comanche sank to the ground with two shafts protruding from his side and died with a blood-laced fist clutching one of them. Hears-the-Wind's body cooked for a short while in the flames until the weight of his body snuffed out all oxygen, killing the fire. The stench of his roasted torso filled the ravine as Two Bears and his comrades moved down the slope to claim their prize.

At first Annabelle saw the attack as a deliverance. Then she saw the Blackfoot warriors plunging down the slope and realized it was anything but.

"Annabelle," Balfour cried, twisting around despite his broken rib, "what's going on?"

"Blackfoot," she told him bitterly. "They've killed or driven off our captors. They want us and the Comanche's ponies, it seems."

One of the Blackfoot warriors strode over to them and planted himself triumphantly before Annabelle. Powerful-looking and unusually tall for a Blackfoot, he had jet-black and expressionless eyes. His sharp cheekbones and powerful jaws delineated a natural arrogance, an unmistakable pride. But what dominated his face was his prominent beak of a nose. Its wide, thick bone looked strong enough to break a fist— Annabelle's, at any rate. His mouth was a closed trap, wide and thin-lipped and cruel.

Annabelle had seen him before, she realized. At the fort.

"The Comanche call you Sky Woman, but I know you as the woman of Crow Wing," he told her.

During her captivity with the Blackfoot, Annabelle had learned their tongue and understood this warrior's words well enough, and they aroused in her a swift and terrible pang as she was reminded of her dead infant son and the Shoshone warrior she had loved.

69

"I am also Golden Hawk's sister," she replied proudly, "and he will reward you greatly for delivering me and my friend from those filthy Comanches."

"Golden Hawk will not thank me. He will come after you. And I will lift his scalp at last and you will end your days as the wife of the great Blackfoot chief, Two Bears."

"If you are Two Bears, listen. I will not make a good and obedient woman for you or for any Blackfoot warrior. The ways of the whites have spoiled me. I will lie under you without passion and my lips will be cold and bitter. And in the end you will suffer the fate of all those who have challenged my brother's powerful medicine."

Two Bears smiled—if that was what it was—and, bending close, slapped Annabelle on the side of the face with such force that it spun her head around and caused her to plunge forward onto the grass, the sting of it bringing tears to her eyes. She heard Brad manage to struggle to his feet and, turning around, saw him, head down, ram Two Bears in the chest. Two Bears grunted, stumbled back, and then fell awkwardly to the ground.

With quiet ferocity two Blackfoot warriors attacked Balfour, one using a battle ax, the other his knife. Annabelle twisted her face away, crying out in horror as the Indians vented their rage. When she looked back again, Balfour was lying facedown, as still as death.

Two Bears regained his feet, grabbed Annabelle by the arm, and hurled her in the direction of the ponies the fourth member of Two Bears' party had just brought into the ravine. In a moment she was astride one of them, her ankles once again tied together under the pony's belly.

With a triumphant cry, the four Blackfoot rode off with their captive, the sister of the mighty Golden Hawk.

— 6 —

Brad Balfour woke to the pounding of his throbbing head. When he tried to move, there was hardly a breath he could take that did not arouse in him a sharp, convulsive pain. He felt like a pincushion from which all the pins had been removed, leaving only pain in their place.

He pushed upward onto his elbows. Sunlight burst upon his eyes, filtering through the sand that had been ground into his sockets and now clung to his eyelashes. He pawed the sand away. Pain lurched like something alive inside his skull. A wave of dizziness brought nausea.

Gingerly he touched a soft, spongy area at the back of his head. He found a lump. Dried blood coated with sand. There were more than a few. And then he remembered the relentless fusillade of blows driving him into the ground, and the sharp, incredible pain as the Blackfoot thrust his blade repeatedly into his arms and sides. He remembered dimly coiling into a ball and trying to burrow into the ground to escape the maniacal fury of his attackers.

The sun's low placement told him it was early

morning. But for how long had he lain like this, half buried in the gravel beside this stream? Flies buzzed around him. Ground mist hung in pockets over the stream and the sides of the ravine. The air was still and cool and moist. The sun was peering at him from behind a long bank of clouds that reached out almost to the horizon.

When his sickness and dizziness began to ease, Balfour started gnawing on the rawhide strips still binding his wrists. Before he finally managed to free himself, the sun was high in the sky and the flies mercilessly persistent as they settled on the countless puddles of dried blood that speckled his buckskins and darkened the sand under his body.

He sat up, thrust his back against a tree, and looked around, aware of a feverish ache that seemed to hang between himself and the world. Every movement was agony as a result of his countless knife wounds, but apparently nothing too essential had been sliced through and he was able to move all his limbs.

But he had no horse, no weapons, and he was miles from the fort. Even worse, Annabelle was gone.

Brad turned his head to look at the Comanche who had fallen into the fire. What was left of his torso was alive with flies. Abruptly, out of their dark, swarming cloud, a hunched bird lurched, a ribbon of fly-specked skin dangling from its beak. Hearing the sound of claws on stone, Balfour twisted his head and saw, just above him on a rock shelf, startlingly close, two vultures pacing restlessly back and forth, their necks craning. He pushed himself farther away from the ledge. As he did so, a vulture darted from behind the other dead Indian farther down the ravine. Having gorged itself, it now struggled heavily into the air while two more of its filthy companions landed running, then waddled obscenely toward the Indian. There was not much left of this Comanche, and already Brad could see parts of his exposed rib cage.

From the looks of the two dead Comanche, he had been in this ravine for more than a day, perhaps two days. Glancing again at the two vultures on the ledge above him, Balfour realized that they might already have started to poke tentatively at his unconscious form. They certainly appeared unhappy enough when he had stirred and come back to life.

Shuddering at the thought of those carrion birds pecking with their bloody beaks at his exposed flesh while he lay unconscious, he grabbed the tree trunk and hauled himself shakily upright. He stood swaying a moment, waiting for his head to clear, and then began to drag himself out of the ravine, away from the dead bodies and the fetid, fluttering rush of the foul birds. He clawed his way up onto the rock shelf. The smooth stone was split into several big chunks. When he tried to haul himself past it, his left foot slipped and skidded into the hollow between two large slabs.

Too late he heard the hard rattle of warning. Something as solid as a thrown lance struck his leg.

He couldn't believe the pain that rocketed through his body and exploded against the top of his skull. His hair stood on end and his body rocked between hot and cold. Crying out, he collapsed across the rock shelf.

The young rattlesnake dropped to the gravel bank below after striking. Sucking in great gutfuls of air, Balfour watched it writhe into a shadowed recess under a boulder. How could anything that small hit that hard? he wondered.

A chill grabbed his body and shook it.

He heard a slithering movement behind him. He felt despair then, shattering and complete. He couldn't move. His luck had run out.

Hawk leaned close.

"Easy, Brad," he told him. "Easy now. How bad you hurt?"

The sudden relief in Balfour's face turned to agony almost at once. "I've been bit . . . by a rattlesnake!"

Beside Hawk, Joe Meek shook his head unhappily. "Shit," he said. "That ain't good."

"Annabelle. Where's Annabelle?" Hawk asked even as he slit through Balfour's buckskin legging with his bowie and examined the snake bite.

"Gone!"

"With who?"

"Blackfoot. They came on us in the ravine and killed two of the Comanche."

"Blackfoot?" Hawk looked in astonishment at Balfour. It was Comanche sign he and Joe Meek had been following until now, sign left by warriors of the Kwahadi band. There had been no doubt in Hawk's mind of this, for if he knew any Comanche sign, he knew the Kwahadi's, his captors for so many years.

And now Balfour was telling them that Blackfoot had Annabelle.

It didn't make sense. Or did it? Those Blackfoot Annabelle had noticed hanging about the fort might easily have been a part of this business from the very beginning. That would explain the ease with which the Indians had entered the fort and their knowing where Annabelle and he were lodged. It had long since occurred to him that they had mistaken Balfour for himself.

"I don't like the look of that snakebite," muttered Joe.

"Neither do I," said Hawk. He glanced at Balfour. "Set your teeth, Brad," he told the man. "I'm going to slice open that bite to bleed out the poison."

Balfour nodded grimly. "Go ahead," he muttered. "I'm ready."

Balfour's leg muscles quivered as Hawk sliced open the wound. A green mass of putrid blood spurted out of the already-swelling calf, then came the blacker, healthier blood. Hawk heard Brad gasp in pain as he threw his head back and squeezed his eyes shut. His fingers dug into the palms of his hands.

Hawk waited for the blood to grow lighter, then reached for his powder horn.

Balfour looked at him through pain-slitted eyes. "What are you up to now?" he gasped. "You going to shoot off the leg?"

"Gunpowder's best for a rattlesnake bite," Joe told Balfour softly, leaning close. "If you're goin' to walk again, lad, we has to burn it clean now."

"Don't sing out, Balfour," Hawk told him. "There might be more Blackfoot around."

Brad nodded grimly. "Or the Comanche who ran away."

Hawk noted Balfour's words grimly, then said nothing more as he poured the gunpowder into the palm of his hand, a small measure, and sifted it carefully into the open wound. A chill shook Balfour and for a moment he stiffened. Hawk took out his flint. He was forced to scratch it several times before the sparks ignited the powder in a small, hissing explosion. Balfour's body arched high off the ground, only his heels and his shoulders touching earth. Then he collapsed back down again, his eyes closed, barely conscious.

Both Hawk and Joe grinned at each other. Balfour would do. He hadn't uttered a sound.

Hawk stood up and put away his knife and powder horn. Walking some distance from the still unconscious Balfour, he beckoned Joe to join him.

"He'll walk in a couple of days, I think," Hawk told Joe.

"He did fine."

"Take him back to the fort. I'm going on after that Comanche he said escaped. I want to know which Blackfoot tribe has Annabelle."

"Besides," said Joe, "you'll be wantin' to fix 'im before he comes after you again."

"An ounce of prevention, Joe."

"Good luck, hoss."

"Thanks for comin' this far. And take care of Balfour. Annabelle said he had a lot to learn about this country. I think maybe his education has just begun."

Hawk had a pony and his packhorse, but the Comanche ahead of him, judging from the tracks he was leaving, was not doing so well. Astride a horse, a Comanche commands only respect. Afoot, he is a stone-age creature fit only to be pitied.

A full day later Hawk caught sight of the warrior stumbling across a narrow meadow ahead of him. Hawk pulled his pony to a halt and dismounted. Then he called out to the Comanche in his own tongue, his words scathing, suggesting that a Comanche without a horse had no honor and no hope of a glorious death.

The Comanche spun, head lowered, furious.

He held only a rifle and a war hatchet. He was a

fine-looking warrior with heavy, broad shoulders, lean shanks, and a narrow waist. As Hawk walked down a grassy slope toward him, he saw the warrior's chest swell with pride. He was well pleased to have this fighting chance with Golden Hawk. He had come far for this honor and Golden Hawk was not going to cheat him out of it.

About fifty yards from the Comanche, Hawk came to a halt, raised his already primed rifle, aimed carefully, and fired. His shot went deliberately high, since he was hoping to catch the Comanche on the right shoulder. He needed the man wounded, not dead. But the bullet missed completely. With a cold smile, the Comanche raised his own rifle. Hawk watched as the barrel steadied in the Comanche's grasp, waited for an instant, and then ducked swiftly to one side just as the rifle cracked. The bullet slammed into the grass beside him, and when the smoke cleared, Hawk saw the Comanche was racing up the slope toward him.

It was what he wanted.

He flung aside his rifle and Colt. He needed this man alive, perhaps even cut up a little, if he were to get any information from him. Drawing his bowie, he ran to meet the Blackfoot. The two met with furious impact, Hawk's greater weight and speed propelling the Comanche backward and to the ground. They rolled over and over in each other's grasp, Hawk slashing at the Indian, the Comanche doing his best to cut away chunks of Hawk's hide with his hatchet. Still in each other's deadly embrace, they dropped off a grassy ledge into a gully and came down hard under a cutbank.

Less then ten strides from a grizzly and her two cubs.

The bears had apparently been digging at the side of the bank for roots, but the gunfire and the sounds of the struggle in the meadow above them had alerted the mother, and she was in the act of herding her cubs off through the gully when Hawk and the Comanche landed just behind them.

To the grizzly, the danger was now too immediate and unsettling for flight. She spun about and placed herself between the two men and her cubs. Lifting onto her hind legs, her great head bent toward them, she roared out her challenge, then fell forward onto her front paws and charged. Hawk managed to pull free of the Comanche and make for the bank. The Comanche was not so lucky. As Hawk flung himself out of the gully onto the grassy meadow above it, he heard the Indian's muffled cry as the grizzly caught him from behind.

Hawk ran across the meadow to where he had left his rifle. Snatching it up, he checked its load, then raced back to the edge of the gully and peered down. The Comanche was lying on his stomach, his head wedged behind a boulder. The bear was leaning over him, woofing and cuffing angrily at the slack, bleeding torso beneath her. Hawk flung up his rifle, aimed at the bear's head just below her ear, and fired. The bear was turning her head when the slug pounded into her skull. A chunk of fur and bone flew up and blood spurted from the wound, but the bear's sudden movement had prevented the bullet from penetrating deep enough to bring her down.

Howling out her rage, the grizzly left the Comanche, turned about, and clawed her way up the cutbank after Hawk with dismaying speed. Running from the gully's edge, Hawk poured powder down the rifle barrel and followed it with a lead ball. By the time he had the load seated and had turned about to lift the Hawken's butt to his shoulder, the bear had reached the clearing and was only twenty yards away. Hawk fired and saw the ball explode into the bear's chest, right over the heart. The grizzly staggered as the half-ounce ball of lead smashed into her. As suddenly as if the bullet had sliced through a puppet master's strings, the bear's feet collapsed, her bloody muzzle plowed through the grass, and she rolled over onto her back, uttering a faint, surprised *whuff*!

Hawk ran closer, his Colt out, and pointed it down at her as a precaution. But she was finally dead and Hawk pushed his Colt back into his belt. She sure as hell had been game enough, and all Hawk felt for the magnificent beast was a deep, reverent awe.

He left the bear and dropped into the gully beside the nearly dead Comanche. The two cubs were gone, he noticed as he pulled the mauled Comanche over onto his back. The Indian's eyes opened.

"You're a dead Comanche," Hawk said in the Comanche tongue. "Who are you?"

"I am Sky Pony."

"You took my sister. Where is she now? Who has taken her?"

"You are Golden Hawk, is that not so?"

"It is."

"The other one with your sister, we think he was Golden Hawk. We take wrong white man."

"There are many blond white men. You are a fool. You came far for Golden Hawk and mistook another for me."

"It is true, this Comanche is a fool. But I will have your scalp. I am not dead yet, Golden Hawk," the unhappy warrior spat. His bravado was impressive, but futile.

Hawk smiled coldly. "You are not dead yet, Sky Pony. That is true. But you soon will be. Most of your leg is gone and there is a hole in your back. Already the flies crawl in to plant maggots inside your body. I do not think you will take Golden Hawk's scalp now. It is over for you. So tell me. Which Blackfoot has taken my sister?"

"I will not tell you."

"This Blackfoot betrayed you. And still you will not tell me."

"You speak like a white man. Your words make no sense."

"Is the Comanche warrior stupid that he does not realize the Blackfoot who killed his comrades and took my sister is the same Blackfoot warrior who guided him to the fort?"

Though this was only a shewd guess on Hawk's part, when he saw the pure dismay register on the Comanche's face, he knew his version of what had happened was more than likely the truth. It explained much, for both men.

"I do not believe you," Sky Pony said, but his tone belied his words. He knew Hawk had discovered the truth.

Hawk shrugged. "Then do not believe me. It does not matter. It is your choice to make. But tell me which Blackfoot took you to the fort, and Golden Hawk will be your friend."

"Friend?"

"Yes."

The Indian snorted contemptuously. "Golden Hawk is not the friend of Sky Pony."

"Listen, Sky Pony. If Golden Hawk is your enemy, he will not kill you. He will let you lie here and rot. Sky Pony's death will come slowly. For many days and nights will he twist in agony. The wolves and bears will visit in the night to tear and rip at him. And when at last Sky Pony's spirit enters the next world, he will have no legs and great, seeping holes in his body pulsing with maggots. He might even be without his scalp."

Sky Pony was in great pain, so great that with each spasm, he was forced to suck in his breath convulsively. His face glistened with cold sweat. Death would be indeed sweet, if it came now, and swiftly. And he knew that Golden Hawk, of all the enemies of the Comanche, spoke the truth.

"Then friend Golden Hawk will kill Sky Pony?"

"Yes, and quickly."

"And you will not take his scalp?"

"I will not take it."

"Perhaps Golden Hawk is a great warrior, after all. Kill me, then. And do it quickly. I can feel the flies crawling deep into my wounds."

"Give me the name of the Blackfoot."

"Two Bears."

"Of which band?"

"The Yellow Blanket Band. Now kill me."

Hawk stood up and took out his Colt. The warrior looked gratefully, unflinchingly up at Hawk. Hawk aimed quickly and fired. The bullet punched a neat hole between the Comanche's eyes, sending him on his way, more or less intact, to a place filled with more game, more buffalo, than he could ever hunt.

Hawk left the gully and hurried back up the slope to his waiting horse.

Gar Trimm had been making plans of his own when Two Bears and his three Blackfoot companions made their move on Sky Pony. By that time he had realized that the chief of the Comanche war party had mistaken the young fool Balfour for Golden Hawk.

Gar did not let this bother him any. It was the woman he wanted, and now, as he crouched behind a screen of juniper—less than ten feet from Two Bear's campfire—he carefully placed his loaded pistol down on the grass beside him.

The members of the Blackfoot war party were taking turns. Two Bears and another Blackfoot had already taken their fill of the woman and were pulling up their breechclouts. Another was grunting heavily as he rutted, while the fourth stood with his back to Gar while he awaited his turn. He was so impatient he had already dropped his breechclout. Beneath the third Comanche the woman, her face turned to one side, lay as unresponding as a log, enduring the humiliation without a sound. She was a tough one, for sure.

Gar brought around his rifle and set it down alongside the revolver. It too was freshly loaded. Then, the blade snicking softly, he withdrew his knife from its sheath, raised it behind his right ear, stood up, and sent it flying. The blade sank deep into the waiting Blackfoot's back, squarely between his shoulder blades. As the Indian sagged forward, Two Bears turned to face his new enemy.

But Gar was already back down behind the junipers. Snatching up his pistol, he shot through the branches, cutting down the Blackfoot standing next to Two Bears. Two Bears leapt across the campfire and headed for the nearby stream. Standing up, Gar tracked him with his rifle and squeezed the trigger. The Indian began to stagger, like a wagon with one of its wheels gone, then collapsed facedown into the water and was immediately caught up in the swift current.

The Blackfoot on top of the woman had already sprung to his feet and run off, as naked as a plucked chicken. Gar stepped out of the junipers, striding over the still-prostrate woman and ramming a fresh load down the rifle's muzzle as he moved. Lifting the rifle swiftly, he placed a round in the fleeing Indian's back. The half-inch ball of lead punched the Blackfoot so powerfully he was sent reeling headfirst into a massive pine, shattering his skull.

Gar looked down at the woman. She was sitting up, her arms folded over her bared breasts, her eyes searching him to see what his motive was. She was not one to trust anyone, not at this stage, at any rate.

"Get dressed," Gar told her. "I have horses. We'd best get free of these heathen bastards."

She did not have to be told twice. She jumped up and in less than twenty minutes they were on their way, trailed by a single packhorse, heavily laden. As soon as they were out of sight of the secluded valley where the Blackfoot had stopped to take their pleasure, Annabelle spurred her horse alongside Gar.

"Thank God," she said, peering at him carefully, trying to remember where she might have seen him before. "I don't know who you are, but . . ." A single tear of gratitude coursed down her cheek. "Thank God for you."

Gar grunted, saying nothing. He was pleased with himself and more than a little anxious at the same time. What he had witnessed from behind that screen of juniper had not angered him. What it had done to him, in fact, was arouse him, and he felt like a wolf in heat. Up close, Golden Hawk's sister was even more beautiful than she had seemed when striding into the fort beside her brother—and this despite her miserable appearance. Her face was bruised and smudged, and her long golden hair had become filthy, dark strands. It was the blue eyes, he realized. They reminded him of his mother's and the realization was like a sharp knife slipping into his heart.

"My name is Annabelle Merriwether," the woman said. "I was taken from Fort Hall by Comanche, then captured by these Blackfoot. It is my brother they want. Jed Thompson."

"You mean Golden Hawk."

"You know him?"

"Yes."

"Who are you?"

"Gar Trimm."

"I'm grateful to you, Mr. Trimm. You can't know how much. My husband will reward you, that I can promise. And to have Golden Hawk as an ally will bring you much honor in this land."

Trimm's blue eyes narrowed as he turned his head to gaze more intently at her than he had allowed himself to before. "Honor I don't want. Not from Golden Hawk, nor from your husband. You're my wife now. I just took you in fair battle, and you can't give me no less'n you gave them heathen savages back there."

"Gave them!"

"They took you, good and proper. You knows the ways of a man. That's clear enough for this child."

She stared at him, having difficulty comprehending the man. "You don't understand. I am a married woman. A white woman. You know what that means. My husband is alive. And so is my brother. Golden Hawk. He'll be coming for me."

"He'll have a fine time findin' you—searchin' after them Comanche, thinkin' yer with 'em." Gar chuckled. "Now shut up and do as I say. The sooner you larn that, the better it'll be. I didn't take you from them Blackfoot to turn you back over to that fort."

The woman was looking at him strangely. "I remember you now," she gasped. "At the fort. You were on the stairs looking down at me. I saw your eyes then."

"You saw me lookin' at you, and that's a fact. Now you jest better get used to the idea. You won't be livin' with no cotton-shirt dandy. I'm your husband now."

He kept on, but she pulled up, her face cold in anger. He pulled up also and turned to look at her.

"I'll never be your wife, Mr. Trimm. You better face up to that here and now. You can take me with you, and I daresay you can make me do whatever you want. But I've lived with the Comanche and the Blackfoot, and I have loved a Shoshone brave and borne him a son. I can live with you if I have to, but you had better not turn your back on me. Ever!"

"That was a pretty speech, sure enough," Gar said, his voice rumbling now with impatience. "Now, we got a few hours before sundown, so we best get ridin'."

"I'm not going with you!"

He laughed, turned his horse, and kept on, leading the packhorse past her. He did not look back. She glanced around her at the nearly impenetrable wilderness. She had no idea where she was, or how far it was to the fort. She had no weapons, no food, her dress was in tatters, and on her feet there were only the remnants of her night slippers.

Helpless, sick at heart, she urged her horse after Gar. She knew she could not survive alone. But she would not give herself to this wild-looking mountain man and she was determined she would make him wish he had never known her. And when her brother Jed found them, as she knew he would, he would kill this man for her.

It was a prayer she would utter every night before sleep.

Then, in a massive, engulfing tide of despair, she thought of her husband, James, already on his way out here to join her, and began to weep openly, unashamedly. Until that moment the fierce anger she had felt at her abduction had kept her from this. But the unbidden image of James had nudged her over the edge.

He was such a proud man, and he loved her so much. When some of his wealthy acquaintances back East had taunted him, ever so slyly, for his having married a woman who had once willingly lived with the Shoshone, he had come to her defense with splendid pride and love, a love he showered on her without stint.

But was there to be no end to his shame?

— 7 —

For two weeks Hawk kept hidden in the timbered foothills surrounding the Yellow Blanket Band of Blackfoot. They were camped on a narrow tributary of the Missouri, in a high-walled valley that opened up onto a fine pasturage for their ponies.

From all that Hawk could gather, the Blackfoot band had been at this campsite for more than a month, but judging from the little amount of meat left on the racks outside their lodges, there would need to be at least one more buffalo hunt before the band moved to their winter camp. During Hawk's vigil he had seen war parties returning from the Crow and Nez Percé lands to the south and west, the braves riding into the village amid great rejoicing, displaying fresh scalps and usually driving before them handsome ponies they had managed to steal. From the Nez Percé, Hawk noted, a sizable band of Appaloosas had been taken, ponies that would be of great value during the upcoming buffalo hunt.

But there was no sign of Annabelle in the village, though there was a dark-haired white woman captive and two older white men, both French *engagés* from their dress. One of the *engagés* had moved in with a large, outsized Blackfoot woman and her white-haired mother, while the other seemed to move about the village with absolute freedom, attracting packs of dogs and Blackfoot children, who apparently found great delight in tormenting him. More than once he saw the exasperated Frenchman hurling sticks or stones—and sometimes horse dung—at his tormentors. This would usually bring out the women of the village, who would gleefully join forces with the children and dogs to put down the Frenchman's rebellion. At such times the other Frenchman kept out of sight, unwilling, it seemed, to get involved in his fellow countryman's trouble.

Meanwhile, Hawk camped on the other side of a distant ridge at the bottom of a narrow ravine well-hidden from prying eyes. Every morning he returned to his surveillance of the Indian village, staying until the last dog had barked, hoping for a sign of the return of Two Bears' war party. But day melted into day and still there was no sign of the Blackfoot war chief . . . or of Annabelle. At last, when Hawk caught unmistakable signs that the Blackfoot village would soon be striking their lodges and moving out for the last buffalo hunt of the season, he determined he would have to enter the village and find out what he could of the missing Two Bears and his war party.

Hawk knew well enough that Two Bears' inexplicable delay in returning to his village with Annabelle might well mean more trouble—or worse—for Annabelle, but he kept this anxious realization at bay by thrusting it deep within him. He had long since learned that, where Annabelle was concerned, he should never lose hope.

As soon as it was dark enough, he left the ledge

where he had crouched for most of the day, dropped to a game trail, and padded along it until he reached the river flowing beside the village. Carrying only the bowie and his throwing knife in its sheath at the nape of his neck, he strode silently into the water until it reached his chin, then dived forward under the water, kicking his feet vigorously and emerging at last near the far shore. He swam toward a clump of birch and climbed out of the water, dripping from every pore, keeping the birch trees between him and the nearest lodge.

Close about this lodge the unattached Frenchman had been seen most frequently by Hawk, and though it was clear that the *engagé* did not live in it, he apparently received comfort and some food from those Indians whose lodge it was. A hearth fire still glowed from within, turning the bottom of the tepee into a huge, softly shining lantern. Hawk waited a decent interval for the water to stop streaming off him, then strode up the bank to the rear of the lodge. Carefully lifting the skirt, he peeped inside and found himself looking at the back of a reclining woman's head. The still-blazing hearth fire gave considerable light, and he could see an old man asleep on the other side of the lodge.

The woman turned. Her eyes were open and they stared without surprise directly into Hawk's. It was the dark-haired white woman Hawk had seen moving about the camp. That afternoon he had seen her washing clothes in the stream. She was Spanish, as he had surmised. He was reminded of his first woman, the Comanche Raven Woman. The moment passed swiftly, however, as he realized how much unlike Raven Woman this particular Spanish captive was. Even with her back to the light he could see enough of her face to admire its beautiful symmetry, and her large, opalescent eyes, as dark as a hidden pool—and just as cool. She looked deep into his eyes without uttering a sound. Then, slowly, she placed a finger to her lips, then pointed in the direction of the tepee's entrance flap.

Hawk lowered the tepee's skirt and moved around to the entrance just as the woman slipped out of the lodge. She wore the remnants of a tattered, ankle-length dress, and he could not help but notice the woman's mature thighs and narrow waist.

Her liquid eyes grew bright with hope as Hawk took her by the hand and drew her away from the lodge and into the water. She shuddered once as the river's cold waters swirled around her, but she did not pull back as Hawk led her deeper into the water and behind the birch clump.

"Who are you?" the woman asked eagerly, her teeth chattering slightly.

"Golden Hawk."

"Yes! I have heard of you. These Blackfoot, they talk much of Golden Hawk and his powerful medicine."

"And the Great Cannibal Owl?"

She shuddered. "Yes! Is it true that you can become like this terrible bird?"

He smiled at her apparent credulity. "Of course it is true. Do you think the Blackfoot would lie about such things?"

She caught the mockery in his tone. "You are just a man, then?"

"Like any other."

"No, I do not think you are like any other."

"Tell me, woman, how are you called?"

"I am Ana Dolores Silva."

"How'd these Blackfoot get a hold of you?"

"It was the Comanche who do this. They raid my husband's freight wagons. He put up fine fight, kill many Comanche. I kill one myself, I think. But he is soon dead, the Comanche do terrible things to him, and I am take captive."

"How'd you end up with this Blackfoot band?"

"I am not happy to be woman of Comanche, so Comanche sell me to this old Blackfoot chief for many fine, spotted ponies. The old chief, with me he try to be young man again. I do all I can to help him, but it is hopeless, so now I take care of him like many years before when I take care of my old father in Santa Fe."

"I need your help, Ana Dolores."

She moved eagerly closer to him. Despite the nearly frigid water, he could feel her sultry warmth. "Hawk, you get me out of this place and I will give you more than help."

Swiftly, Hawk told Ana Dolores of his sister Annabelle and the mauled Comanche's story that she had been taken by Two Bears, a Blackfoot war chief of this Yellow Blanket Band. Then he asked her if there had been any talk of the chief, any family members worried about his being gone so long.

"Yes," she told him emphatically. "There has been much talk. His father, a great old chief, is very worried. But no one knows where Two Bears go. He not tell of his plans when he leave."

Hawk nodded, relieved. This was Two Bears' band, then, and he had not yet returned from his last raid.

"All right," Hawk told Ana Dolores. "Let's take this one step at a time. This Frenchman I've been watching, the one who's been wandering through the village, do you think he might know anything more?"

She shrugged. "Ask him."

"Where is he?"

"He sleeps under big tree. It is his favorite place. And all day he go wherever he like. The Blackfoot let him do as he please."

"Why?"

"He save Indian chief's little girl from drown. Now he is great hero to them. Only he cannot leave. The chief is afraid his little girl will drown if he go from here."

"How is he called?"

"He say his name is René, but the Blackfoot call him Black Fish."

"Can you bring him here? I want to talk to him."

"Sure. I can get him." She smiled quickly. "He would follow me anywhere, that Frenchman."

"Then get him for me."

"Wait here. Do not go away. Remember, you say you take me from this place."

"You have my word."

Her brilliant white teeth flashed in her dusky face. Then she splashed back to the bank, climbed it and disappeared into the darkness beyond the file of lodges lining the river. He did not have long to wait. She returned almost immediately with the Frenchman and he plunged into the water eagerly after her. In a moment they had reached his side behind the birches.

"I am Golden Hawk," Hawk said, shaking the man's hand. The Frenchman's grasp was powerful.

"I am René. What do you do here, English?"

Hawk told him.

"Yes, this Two Bears would do such a thing," René told Hawk. "He would trick the Comanche to get you and your sister. There is always much talk about the fires at night, English. Much brave talk about how they will take the scalp of the terrible Golden Hawk. It is empty talk, fit only for the ears of the women. But Two Bears is fine warrior. He not just talk. He get what he come after, I think. It was Two Bears take my traps and all my beaver and make René slave. But I am lucky. He do not kill me. And now I am famous to these savages. They call me Black Fish."

"You want to stay here, do you, and remain Black Fish?"

René spat into the water swirling past his shoulder and shook his head vigorously, his raggedly cut locks gleaming in the moonlight, his eyes flashing with anger. "I go with you, English, but first, maybe I burn every stinking lodge and all the dogs and children. It is a tribe I hate, I tell you."

René's sudden vehemence was surprising, but understandable. After all, Hawk had once lived himself as a slave among the Comanche. And he had witnessed these past two weeks the systematic torment visited upon René by the Blackfoot women and children, not to mention their flea-ridden curs. Where this Blackfoot band was concerned, René would make an excellent ally.

"What about the other Frenchman?"

"Jacques? That one!" snorted René in disgust. "He has found a home among these devils. Besides, his woman would not let him go. She would kill him first. Then eat him."

Hawk looked at Ana Dolores. She nodded swiftly in confirmation, not so much that Jacques' woman would eat him, but only that she was a terror from which the Frenchman could not easily disengage himself.

"All right, then," Hawk told them. "We'll go now.

I just wish I had some idea of what might have happened to Two Bears."

"Then wait a few more days," René told him.

"Why?"

"The father of Two Bears send Small Fox after Two Bears. Small Fox is only Blackfoot who knows where Two Bears go."

"How long has Small Fox been gone?"

"More than a week."

"I'll wait, then."

"You not take me with you now?" Ana Dolores demanded. Her eyes were wide in dismay. It was apparent she had not counted on staying another night with her old Blackfoot master.

"No," he told her, "not now. We wait . . . until Small Fox returns." He looked at René. "The Blackfoot are making ready for a buffalo hunt, I see."

René nodded.

"But they won't pull out until Small Fox returns."

"I do not think so. But they will not wait much longer, I think."

"Then Small Fox should be returning soon."

"If he find Two Bears—and if he is not dead from other Indian. The Blackfoot, they are not well-liked."

Hawk smiled grimly. *"Not well liked"* was putting it mildly. The Blackfoot tribes were the most hated and feared Indians in this region. He looked at Ana Dolores. "You better return to your lodge, Ana, before your husband finds you missing."

"I do not care," she hissed. "Let him wonder."

"It won't help us to cause a commotion now," he warned.

She took a deep breath. "I stay out here with you this night. I will not go back!"

René's eyes and teeth gleamed in appreciation of Ana Dolores' determination and need. He looked at Hawk. "Maybe you better not argue with this one, English. She has hot temper. I know, for many times have I tried to take her."

Hawk was in a quandary, but it was soon resolved, and with a suddenness that almost brought disaster. Looking past the two of them, he saw an old Indian, cadaverous in the extreme, striding into the water. He was naked, except for a blanket thrown over one shoulder, and in his hands he was holding an ancient flintlock. Hawk did not have to be told whom this irate old man was coming after.

Catching Hawk's glance, René turned his head. "*Merde . . .*" he muttered.

Whirling about, Ana Dolores saw her husband approaching and gasped, then pushed herself rapidly through the water toward him. The old Indian pulled up, raised his rifle, and fired point-blank at her. There was a muffled explosion as the flint ignited the powder in the pan, but there was no detonation, only a sudden dense cloud of smoke coiling about the old man's head and shoulders.

He raised the rifle over his head to club Ana Dolores, but she swept in under his upraised arms and, with a small, wicked cry of triumph, grabbed him about the neck and bore him backward and down beneath her. Hawk watched in astonishment as they both disappeared under the water. He began striding through the water toward them when Ana Dolores popped back up and flung her wet hair back over her shoulders, turning to face him and René.

"The old bag of bones is dead," she cried in grim triumph.

The flintlock rifle had not fired its round, but the stiffled explosion that came when the powder had caught had been loud enough to arouse the village. A single dog, barking fiercely, was racing along the bank, and three or four Indians bearing torches were streaming through the village toward the river.

Ana Dolores' husband had decided the issue. She would not be staying another night in the Blackfoot village.

"Swim," Hawk told them. "I have a camp and horses on the other side of that ridge."

He did not need to say anything more.

When they reached Hawk's camp, René took Hawk's rifle and climbed onto the ravine's rim to keep a lookout as the Blackfoot warriors slipped back and forth through the timber searching for them. But Hawk had chosen his campsite well amd the sounds of the searchers gradually faded.

The icy water had penetrated every stitch of Hawk's buckskins, and as he sat in the darkness beside Ana Dolores, the cruel dampness entered every curve of his body, transmitting a numbing chill deep into his bones. His teeth began to chatter finally, and a moment later he felt Ana Dolores' fingers lift the flap of his buckskin shirt over his head. He put down his Colt and helped her and saw as he did so that she had already taken her clothes off. In a moment she had him stripped naked. He turned to her, the pine needles scratching his buttocks.

Her dark face leaned close to his, and before he could protest—if protest was what he had in mind— she had covered him with her own glowing body, drawing the chill from his bones as if by magic.

"We are both cold from that river," she whispered huskily. "Now we will warm each other."

He lay back and reached up his arms to enclose her. She snuggled down onto him and laughed softly, her lips closing happily about his, while the warmth of her continued to fill him, the way hot coffee on a chill morning warms the soul.

"That foolish old Indian, he beat me because I cannot make him a man," she told him softly, her hot breath fanning his right ear. "But it was not me. I try everything, and still it was no good. With you, Hawk, I do not need to try so hard."

"Yes," he agreed. "It is enough we are together."

"Yes. Oh, yes, Hawk," she cried softly, feeling him then. "It is. It truly is."

He stopped the movement of her lips by enclosing them with his own. Still holding them, he rolled over gently onto her and, thrusting deeply, gently, entered her.

And she was right. Despite everything, at that moment it was enough that they were together.

Two days later, many miles south of the Blackfoot village, the three of them watched two Indians riding toward them across a long, gently rising meadow.

Crouching in the tall grass beside Hawk, René nodded in response to Hawk's query of a moment before.

"Yes," he said. "It is Small Fox. The other one is Two Bears, I think."

"He does not ride well," Ana Dolores commented. "He rides like an old woman."

"He rides like someone with a bullet in him," Hawk said after a moment, "and that explains a lot."

"I do not see your sister," said Ana Dolores.

"Nor do I," admitted a troubled Hawk.

"Perhaps she is safe at Fort Hall," René suggested hopefully. "We will be there soon and find her. Then all will be well and you will be a very happy man."

"Nothing good comes easy," Hawk told him. "No, I do not like this. We will have to capture these two and find out what happened to my sister."

"How do we do that?"

"Listen," Hawk said, "and I will tell you."

When the two Indians crested the meadow, a voice called to them from a clump of timber off to their right. They halted their ponies and turned to look in that direction. What they saw were two riders, both of them familiar, break from the timber and ride slowly toward them. Small Fox held up his hand in puzzled greeting as Ana Dolores and René approached them.

"You are far from the village," Small Fox noted cautiously. It was obvious to him that the two had run off, and this did not please him. But he had other matters to deal with now, and was impatient to be on his way.

Ana Dolores pulled her pony to a halt and looked at the Blackfoot riding beside Small Fox. The Indian had sagged forward over his pony's neck the moment they halted, and now he did not even bother to turn his head to gaze at her or at René. He was a very sick Indian.

"What is wrong with Two Bears?" René asked, pulling his pony to a halt a little closer to Small Fox, an ingratiating smile on his swarthy face. His command of the Blackfoot tongue was as good as hers.

"He has been shot. There is a bullet in his back."

"Comanche?"

"A white trapper. A great, giant bear of a man. That is what Two Bears has told me."

"A single white trapper has brought down the famous Two Bears. And he did not ride out alone. What manner of man could this have been?"

For the first time, Small Fox noticed the Colt resting on the pommel of René's saddle. A white man's saddle, he noted at the same time. Ana Dolores shifted her position on the horse she was riding, and Small Fox saw the muzzle of a rifle barrel poke into view. Before he could do anything, a powerful hand caught his long hair from behind and dragged him with ruthless force off his horse. He managed to gasp out loudly a second before he struck the ground; then he landed with such force that all the breath was knocked from his lungs.

That single cry, however, was enough to alert the wounded Two Bears, who stirred himself as if from a deep slumber and kicked his pony in the flanks. But the same hand that had flung Small Fox from his pony grabbed him by the waist and hurled him into the grass. When he hit the ground, the awful pain of it caused him to grunt loudly, then lose consciousness.

As René and Ana Dolores dismounted and covered the dazed Small Fox, Hawk walked over to the unconscious Two Bears and kicked him awake. When Two Bears was fully aware, he shook his head and, despite his condition, took a deep breath and hurled himself upright at Hawk. Hawk took a quick step to one side, caught the Indian's arm, and lifted him off the ground. Then he hurled him through the air. The Indian's head caught the ground first; he jackknifed loosely and came to rest on his back. Trotting over to him, Hawk leaned over the slowly twisting warrior and took the hatchet from his belt. Then he lifted the Indian's bow and arrows off his shoulder. He pulled an arrow from the quiver, and fitting its notch to the bowstring, he pulled back on the string and waited for Two Bears to regain his senses enough to focus on the arrowhead.

When he did, Hawk said quietly, "I will let this arrow bury itself in your heart if you do not tell me what happened to my sister."

"It is true what Small Fox has already told you."

"One man—a trapper—rescued her?"

"Yes." Two Bears' eyes went mean and small. "We were busy with your whore of a sister and did not see him come up."

The words were intended to goad Hawk into a fury, and they succeeded. He stepped forward and kicked the Indian in the chin, sending him arching backward into the grass. It took a moment for Two Bears to recover his senses again.

"This trapper," Hawk prodded. "Who was he?"

"He is the one Golden Hawk and the Nez Percé bring to the fort, the one who lose his woman to the grizzly."

Hawk was astonished. Gar Trimm? Was that possible? Then Hawk recalled René's words of a few minutes before. Hawk would return to Fort Hall, he had suggested, and would find Annabelle already there. Now those words did not seem so impossible. Gar Trimm had repaid a favor, and for this Hawk would be forever grateful.

Slowly, Hawk lowered the bow. He wanted to kill Two Bears for engineering this escapade. It was clear now that Two Bears' use of the Comanche had been a clever ruse to avoid any repercussions to his band for capturing Hawk and his sister, thus enabling the band's members to continue trading at the fort.

It had almost worked.

"You are a dangerous enemy, Two Bears. But I would have let you live had you not dishonored my sister."

Hawk lifted the bow almost casually and let the arrow fly. The shaft crashed through Two Bears' gullet and he gagged to death on his own blood. Slowly.

Hawk turned to Small Fox. The Indian was on his feet, standing by his pony, Ana Dolores and René facing him with drawn weapons. His face was white. He had just seen what had happened to the great war chief of the Yellow Blanket Blackfoot, and he saw no reason why such a fate should not be visited upon him as well.

Hawk turned to Ana Dolores and René. "Tell me of this brave," he said. "Does he deserve to die like that dog of a Blackfoot on the grass over there?"

Ana Dolores frowned in thought. "He was always kind to me," she told Hawk. "Once when my husband beat me, he came into the lodge and scolded him, and that night I slept in peace. It was not much, but it was something."

"When the women would come after me with sticks for their own amusement," said René, "this one would shame them and drive them off. And he never treated me unkindly. He searched for Two Bears because he heard Two Bears' old father wailing in his lodge. It was his good heart that sent him after Two Bears. He felt sorry for the old man."

"What René say is true," agreed Ana Dolores. "Small Fox is a Blackfoot, but he has a good heart."

"Kill me," said Small Fox. "I am not afraid to die.

If you do not kill me, Golden Hawk, I will come after you—and these other two as well. Hear me. I will do this."

"You are a brave warrior and you have a good heart," Hawk told the Blackfoot. "So I will not kill you. But I will shame you, so that you will think twice before coming after Golden Hawk and his comrades."

Stepping forward, Hawk boosted the unhappy brave onto his pony. He tied the Indian's ankles together with a length of rawhide he passed under the pony's belly. Then he tied the brave's wrists securely around the pony's neck. When he got through, the Indian could not get off the pony, nor could he halt or guide it.

Hawk stepped back and nodded to Ana Dolores and René. They brought down their palms on the pony's flanks. The pony leapt forward. Hawk fired his Colt into the air over the pony's head, and the pony appeared to gain wings. In a moment it moved out of sight beyond a distant ridge, its tail flowing straight out behind it.

There was a nip in the air when Hawk and the others finally glimpsed Fort Hall in the distance. Summer was long gone, and the smells and colors of autumn were showing everywhere. Before long, the first snows would cover the high passes and lower peaks of the Great Divide, but Annabelle would be safe here in the fort and all would be well once again.

As they rode onto the long flat in front of the fort, Hawk noticed no Blackfoot lodges were set up outside the fort this time, only Crow and Shoshone tepees. Hawk and his two companions had been visible from the fort for some time, and now its gates swung wide and Hawk saw a tall, familiar figure striding out to greet him.

It was Captain James Merriwether, Annabelle's husband.

Hawk waved and kicked his pony to a trot, but his pleasure at being back faded quickly when he saw the grim, questioning look on Merriwether's face.

Reaching the tall captain, Hawk quickly slipped off his pony. "What is it, James?" he asked, obstinately clinging to the hope that Gar Trimm had already brought Annabelle back to the fort. "Is Annabelle all right?"

"Dammit, Jed," Merriwether replied, "that's what I've come out here to ask you. You've been gone so long. Surely, you must have found her."

"You mean she's not here?"

"My God, Jed! You're the one who went after her. Where is she? I didn't think you'd come back without her."

Hawk turned and looked with sudden dismay at Ana Dolores and René. He had been right the first time. Nothing good comes easy.

— 8 —

The hidden valley to which Gar Trimm took Annabelle was deep in the mountains, far northwest of the Snake. It had been a remote valley when Gar first stumbled upon it many years before, and he had managed to keep its location a secret from those he came upon when hunting outside the valley or trading his plews at the forts. This was not easy, for one glance at the thick, glossy beaver pelts he brought in caused eyebrows to raise. The beaver were running out, the mountain men all complained, and then one look at his haul and they would wonder and begin asking questions.

After his upbringing in the filth of the St. Louis slums, the valley filled Gar from the first with an almost breathless sense of wonder, even reverence, a feeling that had only increased over the years. The valley never disappointed him, nor did it lie. Its slopes and the mountain lake that sat in its embrace were forever clean and fresh, the game abundant. Amazingly, despite the altitude, the climate within the valley was temperate. As a result, it enjoyed milder winters than the more open parklands on the lower slopes, where the cutting winds blew unimpeded and the snowdrifts sometimes piled high enough to bury a man. And when the full force of winter finally broke across the barrier of peaks ringing the valley, the heavy snow was like a benediction as the protective cloak of pristine white covered everything, even the streams rushing off the slopes, while the lake became a vast white tablecloth where occasionally he would track and kill elk caught on its surface or frozen in its shallows.

It did not take him long to begin to think of the valley as belonging to him. No other white man knew these beaver-filled streams and fragrant woods as he did; no one but he gazed into the lake's fabulously clear depths. And since the valley was his, he would allow no man—no other trapper or hunter, and certainly no settler—to claim it from him.

Into this valley he brought Annabelle proudly.

He said not a word to her as they rode into the pass and started down through the timber, the glint of the lake below showing through the trees. He expected the valley's pristine beauty to say what he felt, and it was with deep satisfaction that he noted the undisguised wonder that sprang into the woman's eyes as she gazed about her. During the long journey to the valley, she had been a sullen, bitter woman, profoundly unhappy, not allowing him the slightest liberties, and he was hoping this glimpse of her new home would soften her some and allow him to eventually tame her.

For he saw her now as a wild thing, as elusive as the birds that nested in the pines, as lovely as the does that flitted like tawny shadows through the trees. It would be as difficult to catch her heart, he knew, as it would be to climb a tree and pluck a bluebird in flight. But that made the prospect all the more challenging.

This tall, willowy blond woman would be worth waiting for, worth taming—as he had once tamed a motherless doe.

From the beginning, he had always hated the Indian women who opened their thighs for him without a murmur of protest, who grimaced in naked lust during coupling, and who sometimes astonished and repelled him with their barbaric variations. Nor had he ever been able to gain any satisfaction from the lank, foul-smelling white whores who had serviced him for a pittance when as a young man he ran through the streets of St. Louis.

No, this woman, this sister of the famous Golden Hawk, was what he wanted. She knew men, but she was no whore. And the more he looked into her eyes, the more somber he became, the more thoughtful, and he found himself back in that other time—that brief, hauntingly beautiful time when his mother, a lovely, blue-eyed woman with a voice like an angel, crooned to him and bent to brush his silky hair off his tiny forehead.

Annabelle halted her horse and looked up at the cabin in pure astonishment. Seeing the look on her face, her captor grinned, his yellow teeth flashing in his full beard.

"How d'ya like it?" he asked, his voice no more than a growl. "I built it myself four years gone now."

She knew he was proud of it, that he had been waiting for this moment, and she did not want to please him by showing the surprise and the grudging admiration she felt, but she realized she had already done so.

The cabin sat on the edge of a clearing in front of a

great slab of granite that seemed to have been sliced
out of the mountainside looming above it. The clearing was small, and it was not visible from any other
point on the slope, so that when their horses broke
into the clearing and Annabelle saw the cabin, its
sudden appearance astonished her, as much by the
sight of a man-made structure in this high, nearly
impenetrable wilderness as by its spaciousness, its impressive solidity. It was a fortress against the world,
she realized, and in that instant she understood more
than she cared to about Gar Trimm, the mountain
man who had abducted her.

There was a barn behind the cabin for their horses,
and after the animals were relieved of their burdens,
watered, and given their ration of oats, Gar Trimm
escorted her into the cabin. The interior was what she
had expected from the exterior—solid, serviceable.
The fireplace covered the northern wall, and the hearth
was large enough for her to be able to walk into it.
Great metal hooks swung out from the fieldstone, and
from the hooks dangled large, cast-iron pots.

The table and chairs were all constructed from rough-
cut pine, but the tabletop had been planed to an
amazingly smooth finish. There were two bedrooms
off the main living room, and the kitchen was off to
the right of the fireplace. Looking about her, she felt
much as she imagined Goldilocks must have felt when
she found herself in the house of the three bears.

Only this was no fairy tale.

"My bed's in there," Gar told her, pointing to the
largest of the two bedrooms. "You kin sleep in the
other room if you've a mind."

This surprised—and pleased—Annabelle. She blushed

in gratitude as she nodded her thanks. "Yes," she told him. "I'll sleep in there. But I have few things."

"There's a trunk at the foot of your bed. My Indian woman put her things in there. They'll do for now. You're taller'n she was."

Annabelle nodded and hurried into the room. Pleased to find a door, she gently closed it and sat down on the heavily quilted bed and closed her eyes, her heart racing. She was in turmoil, for this was to be her new home and Gar Trimm was to be her husband. This he had made perfectly clear. But how was it, then, that he was treating her like this now? It was almost more than she could bear—this uncertainty.

For she had expected that, once inside the four walls of his cabin, Gar would fall upon her like some mad, ravening animal. That, at least, was how her grim imagination had pictured it. What was happening instead was disquieting, but only because she was so unprepared for it. Now, for the first time since her capture by the mountain man, as she sat on the edge of the bed with her hands clasped prayerfully before her, hope—as tentative as a chick breaking through its shell—nudged itself to life within her.

For two weeks after Hawk returned to the fort, he and Annabelle's husband searched the mountains near the spot where Hawk and Tames Horses had come upon Gar and the grizzly, tramping up and down streams Gar might have trapped. In gradually widening arcs, they circled the spot, entering Shoshone, Bannock, and Nez Percé villages in the course of their search. In each case, once the purpose of Hawk's visit was made clear, Hawk and Merriwether found themselves greeted cordially by the Indians. Golden Hawk, it seemed, might be a fearsome enemy, but as a guest, each village vied for the honor of providing him and his companion genuine hospitality.

Nevertheless, not one Indian stepped forward with news of Gar's whereabouts. It was as if he and Annabelle had vanished off the face of the earth. Discouraged, with a troop of government dragoons and surveyors waiting impatiently back at Fort Hall, Merriwether returned to the fort to try a southern route to California, since it was now too late in the season to scout a route through the mountains to Oregon. Though Merriwether was reluctant to leave, Hawk convinced him that he had no choice but to honor the commission he had been given by the U.S. government, not to mention the lives and fortunes of those in his party who had come this far to carry out the task. At the same time Hawk assured Merriwether that until the snow made travel through the mountains impossible, he would continue his search for Annabelle.

Merriwether and his party left Fort Hall, Joe Meek guiding them toward the Humbolt River, and alone now, Hawk rode deeper into the mountains, continuing his search. In his anxiety for his sister's safety, he ignored his own good sense, and when the first snows of winter whitened the meadows and began filling up the higher mountain passes, he kept going, searching along every stream, seeking out every Indian encampment.

But at last he saw the futility—and the danger—of continuing his search alone with winter's brutal cold threatening, and on one bright cold morning he started on the long journey back to Fort Hall.

*　　*　　*

A week later Hawk awoke to find himself staring up at a Blackfoot Indian. He did not know the warrior, but from the war paint on his chest and the ribbons on his feathered headpiece, Hawk knew him to be a Blood Indian from a distant band close to the Canadian border. Whoever he was, Hawk knew he had not journeyed this distance to give Hawk news of Annabelle's whereabouts.

He had come this far to kill Hawk.

Over his head the Blackfoot held a lance, and his feet were poised so that he could send it into Hawk's heart without shifting his weight. His craggy face broke into a grim smile when he saw Hawk blinking up at him.

"The medicine of Black Elk is great," he told Hawk.

"I'm glad to hear that, Chief."

"This warrior travel many days through the lands of his enemies. He seeks sign that the buffalo hunt will be successful and that the spotted sickness will not strike his people again."

Hawk listened, but he was tensing himself, preparing to make an upward lunge, even though he knew that his chances of escaping the poised lance were close to zero. Smiling, Hawk nodded to encourage the Indian to keep on talking.

"And now," continued Black Elk, "the gods present Black Elk with a momentous sign, a great trophy. Black Elk will bring back the skull of the famed Golden Hawk."

"That will sure be a great sign," agreed Hawk.

"Black Elk will be very famous. No more will his people be ravaged by Golden Hawk and the Great Cannibal Owl."

"You know what, Black Elk?" Hawk said. "You talk too much."

Even as he spoke, Hawk uncoiled from the ground. Falling back in astonishment, the Blood warrior flung his lance. Its long steel tip sliced into Hawk's side, but Hawk was now a raging thunderbolt of destruction. His knife slashing, he bore Black Elk to the ground beneath him and, with a series of terrible, merciless thrusts, slashed the warrior's heaving chest into bloody shreds. Again and again he plunged his bowie's blade deep into the dying warrior, and was still lifting the blade over his head when he toppled to one side and and for a moment or two lost consciousness.

Flies were already buzzing about him when he pulled himself away from the dead Indian. Staggering to his feet, he took strips of rawhide from his saddlebag and wound them about the gash in his side, tightening the rawhide painfully until the flow of blood was stanched. Then he mounted up, turned his horse south, and continued on to Fort Hall.

A day later he awoke chilled to the bone. The mountains seemed to have lifted themselves overnight into a rare and much colder altitude. By the time he broke camp, snow was falling and a wind from the north was stinging his face raw. He mounted up carefully and set out. The wound in his side was growing more troublesome. Something deep and vital had been violated. No matter how tight he kept the rawhide, he was unable to stem the dark stream that oozed from it. And the growing pain was like a terrible vice closing about his waist.

Now, as he followed the dim trail ahead of him, he became aware of how incredibly cold it had become. The snow was flying at him on the wings of a fierce wind. There was no doubt about it; this blizzard was the beginning of the high country's winter.

Soon the ground ahead of him was white, and the trees bordering the trail faded into ghostly presences only dimly perceived through the swirling snow. The tiny flakes stabbed painfully at his eyes, causing the world to explode into multicolored lights. Hawk had tied his hat on with a piece of rawhide and he had put on his wolfskin jacket. But in this bitter cold, the jacket offered only minimal protection from the demented wind that tore at him from first one side and then the other. His buckskin leggings, meanwhile, had become stiff, unyielding encasements of ice that clasped his thighs in their cold grasp.

Whenever a clump of trees afforded him enough shelter, he would stop and give himself and his horse a chance to recover, and in this halting, miserable fashion he was able to keep going throughout the day. Night found him camped in a rough lean-to he fashioned from pine and birch branches, with a howling wind at his back and a campfire that gave off only a whisper of warmth. He was feverish and slept only fitfully, and as the night wore on, the wind wailed about his little shelter with even greater savagery.

Morning came with no sign that the storm, bent on transforming the world into a bastion of snow and ice, was letting up. As Hawk rode on, the snow-laden wind cut at him like thousands of tiny knives, shriveling his flesh and threatening to wither his soul. It sliced beneath the wolfskin jacket, cut through his flesh, and stabbed at his bones. It froze the hair in his nose and iced the snout of his horse, turning the leak of its nostrils into frosty daggers.

At last the trail began to dip and he knew he was

leaving the mountains behind. He had been waiting for this, believing the storm's fury would surely abate once he left the high country. Incredibly, the lower altitude seemed to have no effect on the storm. If anything, its strength only seemed to increase.

Again he camped in among pines, huddled in another clumsily fashioned lean-to. Overhead, the snow swirled blindingly. There was not a hint of the moon or stars. The wind in the pines' branches screeched with an intensity that set Hawk's chattering teeth on edge. He inspected his wound by the light of his dim fire and found it—incredibly—alive with maggots. With numbed fingers he tried to clean them from it, but gave up at last and coiled himself about the fire, drawing as close to it as he could get without setting fire to his blankets.

His sleep, when it came, was disordered, fevered. Visions of Annabelle floated before him. She was laughing at one time, weeping at another. For a while, he was back in Cambridge, in a sun-bathed backyard, sipping iced tea and trying to make himself comfortable in a wrought-iron chair while perfumed ladies in expensive silks and bonnets crowded about him, eagerly bombarding with idiot questions the wild, blond warrior from the West they had heard so much about. As the dream faded, Hawk recalled once again with gratitude Annabelle breaking through the ring of chattering females to rescue him.

That was only one of his dreams concerning Annabelle. There were others, and none of them was pleasant; in the last of them, he could hear Annabelle's despairing scream fading before him as he plunged wildly through a dark wood after her. . . .

Hawk awoke in a panic. He was shivering violently.

The fire was out, a black socket in the snow's face staring blindly up at him in the pale light of another day. The blizzard still howled in full fury. He sat up while the snow swirled around him, swaying a little, aware of the maggots crawling in his wound, but aware also that he no longer cared.

He was enormously tired. His eyelids were leaden. The snow had blown in through the lean-to and covered him completely. He let his head sink down again before the intense screaming of the wind. He was in no hurry, he told himself. It would be all right if he just rested awhile longer before mounting up again and continuing his journey through this infernal, howling wall of snow.

He curled into a ball and let his eyes close, waiting for the numbing tide of sleep to bear him away from the awesome, vindictive cold. But the wound in his side, the constant, unremitting chatter of his teeth, and the occasional, violent shudders that racked him simply would not release him to the delicious slumber he craved. At last he raised his head and looked about him. His body had refused to betray him, even if his will to survive had.

"So this is the great Golden Hawk," he said aloud, to rouse himself still more, "sleeping with maggots in his side while he lets a demented mountain man carry off his sister."

He struggled out of his blankets. Like a drunken man he staggered from the lean-to and wallowed about in the waist-deep snow, flailing clumsily at his gear. He managed somehow to saddle the horse, roll up his gear and tie it behind the cantle, and mount up. As he rode off through the white, shrieking world, he trusted himself almost completely to the pony's good sense to continue on down the sloping meadows.

He rode all that day, a white rag doll clinging to the horse, too weak to halt for occasional breaks, since he knew that if he dismounted, he might not be able to pull himself back up into the saddle again. Despite the awesome cold, he was on fire. His left side was encased in a chilling armor of frozen blood that extended well down his thigh. He wanted to stop and make camp, but he realized that if he made camp this night, he would sleep on well past the next dawn . . . into eternity. He had to keep going through the night, until he fell off the horse or the horse collapsed under him.

He became aware that the horse was now moving across a level plain. Not long after this, a black, star-studded window appeared in the clouds of snow swirling about him. The ragged window frame shifted, revealing a towering, pine-stippled butte, resplendent in its new coat of white. Then the wind-whipped clouds swept across his field of vision again, blocking out the stars and the butte.

But that one glimpse had been enough.

Judging from that landmark, Hawk realized he was only a mile at best from Fort Hall. He had only to shift his pony's direction slightly to the southwest. Slowly, carefully, he turned his horse. As he rode, the lacerating wind whipped at his back, searing his unprotected neck with renewed fury. But he ignored it. It was a blue norther he was fighting, but there was a good chance now that he would beat it.

It was a few hours from dawn when Hawk slipped from his horse and reached out for the gate. But the drifts had piled so high against it that he could not open it. He cursed and looked about him. The few remaining Indian lodges were dark, shadowy ghosts lost in the shifting curtains of snow. He turned back to the gate and began pounding on it with the handle of his Colt. When that brought no help, he tried to fire his rifle, but the driving snow prevented the caps from firing even when he was able—at enormous physical cost—to load the muzzle.

He sagged to the ground, amazed and astonished at the irony. To have come this far and failed. It was almost funny. Almost.

His back was wedged securely against the gate, the snow piling up about his shoulders with indecent haste, when he felt the gate shift and begin to push against him. He did his best to move away from the gate. As he did so, the gate opened still farther. He managed to turn. In the gradually widening doorway, he saw Ana Dolores' face.

She was a Spanish snow maiden, her head and shoulders white with snow, her dark eyes glowing. Reaching out, she pulled Hawk through the gate, laughing in relief and triumph.

"I was right," she cried, clasping Hawk to her. "It is you I see, not some bear like they say."

Hawk could not reply. He was too tired. The last thing he remembered was becoming aware of a wonderful, welcome stench, and turning his head, he saw Old Bill Williams plunging toward him through the sheets of snow.

Almost a week after the norther hit, the new snow still shone as brightly as ever to Tames Horses' eyes. Too brightly, in fact. As he peered through the trees, his old eyes were forced to squint.

But he had no difficulty recognizing Gar Trimm. It was the same trapper he and Golden Hawk had rescued from the grizzly, a powerful bull of a man over six feet tall, with arms like tree trunks and dressed in filthy buckskins. Across the front of his chest, Tames Horses could see where Gar had sewn with rawhide the tears in the fabric left by the grizzly's claws, the seams rough but serviceable.

Gar was standing by a large flat rock, cleaning a beaver pelt. He had stretched the pelt out on the rock, fur side down, and with a knife and stone chisel was scraping off every particle of flesh and fat. A small earthenware bowl was sitting in the snow beside Gar, and into this he was dropping the fat and flesh. Tames Horses knew what Gar would do with the bowl's contents; later, they would be boiled into a thick, gelatinous soup. Gar had probably set aside the beaver's brains to give the soup body.

Gar was working so intently, he did not look up when Tames Horses stepped from the timber. But after the Indian had taken only a few strides through the snow, the mountain man flung down his stone chisel and snatched up his rifle, leveling it at Tames Horses.

The old Indian held up his hand, palm out, then halted. "You are Gar, the one who fight the grizzly," Tames Horses reminded him in English. "Do you not remember me? We kill grizzly and bring you to fort."

Slowly, Gar lowered his rifle. "I remember you," he admitted. "What're you doin' here, Chief?"

"This valley, I remember it well. Much game. Much beaver."

"That's so. But this is my valley. You ain't stayin' here, Chief."

Tames Horses thrust out his old chest and flung his head back proudly. "Many times this old chief hunt and trap in this valley. Why you not want me to stay here? There is plenty beaver for Indian and white trapper."

And then Tames Horses saw the woman all the tribes had been talking about—the golden-haired sister of his great friend Golden Hawk—step from the timber and start across the clearing toward them. Her resemblance to Golden Hawk was unmistakable. She had the same tall figure, the blue eyes, the handsome features, and the golden hair. Most of it was hidden by a ragged bonnet, but Tames Horses could see a few golden wisps poking out from under the hat's peak. She was wearing a long black dress and white man's boots wrapped in strips of trade blanket.

Gar turned at her approach, bridling. "Get back to the cabin," he snapped. "You're not needed here."

But she strode on boldly through the snow. "Who is this Indian?" she asked, pretending she hadn't already met him.

"Name's Tames Horses. I'm tellin' him to get out of here. I ain't sharin' this valley's beaver with no one."

Coolly, the golden-haired woman glanced past Gar and greeted Tames Horses in fluent Shoshone, a language with which Tames Horses had more than a passing acquaintance, having had to deal with a Shoshone mother-in-law in his younger days. Tames Horses nodded solemnly at the woman's polite greeting and greeted her in like manner.

"Here, what you doin' there, woman?" the trapper demanded. "It won't do you no good to talk Shoshone to this Indian. He's a Nez Percé."

"It was a simple greeting," she retorted.

"I'm warnin' you, Annabelle. Don't say nothin' more to this redskin."

Ignoring him, she addressed Tames Horses directly, "You are the friend of Golden Hawk. I am his sister. Bring word to him that I am in this valley with this man. He keeps me against my will. Do this and my husband and Golden Hawk will reward you greatly."

She would have said more, but the huge mountain of a man strode angrily through the deep snow to her side and struck her on the side of the head with his clenched fist. The blow sent the woman tumbling back into a drift, and for a moment she disappeared beneath its shiny, crusted surface. When she did manage to sit up and then stand, she brushed herself off with great dignity and fixed the big mountain man with her icy blue eyes.

"Is it a crime to invite an old Indian into our cabin? Surely we can offer him that much hospitality."

Gar frowned in some confusion, then glanced over at the Indian. "Never mind what she told you, Chief. You ain't welcome in this valley and in my cabin. Make tracks or I'll feed your liver to the grizzlies."

"That is very unfriendly," said Tames Horses.

Lifting up his rifle, Gar aimed and fired. The round caught Tames Horses high on his right shoulder, the force of its impact hurling him backward into the snow. Looking up, Tames Horses saw Gar stride closer and spit a fresh ball into his rifle barrel. The mountain man meant to kill him, Tames Horses realized with some surprise. He reached for his knife with his left hand and prepared to sell his life dearly.

But a blond fury drove at Gar from behind, striking him in the small of the back. As Gar dropped the rifle and sprawled awkwardly forward into a drift, Tames Horses got to his feet and headed for the timber. It was heavy going for a man his age, and just as he ducked into the woods, a shot from behind clipped off a low-hanging branch inches from his head.

Once in the woods, he turned and glanced back. Gar had knotted his fist into the woman's hair and was dragging her through the snow. Golden Hawk's sister showed great courage and fought back with undiminished rage, but this only succeeded in arousing the mountain man to such anger that he clubbed her senseless; then, slinging her over one massive shoulder, Gar disappeared in the direction of his cabin, apparently convinced that he could dismiss Tames Horses as a future threat.

It was not a foolish conclusion, based on the bloody trail Tames Horses had left in the snow as he fled the enraged trapper. Once he was deep enough in the trees to pause, Tames Horses slumped onto a boulder and examined his wound. As he had feared, the bullet had smashed through his shoulder and taken much muscle with it. The inside of his buckskin shirt was warm with his blood, and unless he kept moving, it would freeze into a shield of coagulated blood, further restricting the movement of his right arm and shoulder.

He left the boulder and kept moving, heading for the spot where he had left his horse. The news that Hawk was looking for his sister had come to him from a Nez Percé hunter many weeks before. The brave had settled himself comfortably beside the hearth fire in the solitary old warrior's lodge; they had smoked for a while in silence, and then with only passing reference to the buffalo hunt this past fall, the hunter had launched into a story he knew would be of great interest to the old chief, the visit of Golden Hawk to his village.

His voice trembling with subdued excitement, he told Tames Horses that Golden Hawk's sister had been abducted by a mountain man, the same that many Nez Percé knew as Hair Face. The woman's husband was with Hawk and both showed great concern for her safety.

As soon as the brave mentioned Hair Face, Tames Horses realized he was the same trapper he and Golden Hawk knew as Gar Trimm. Later that day, as he waved good-bye to the Nez Percé hunter, Tames Horses recalled the packs of beaver plews the grizzly had torn inside Gar's lodge. The beaver pelts had been prime. Very prime. Once, in a high, distant valley, Tames Horses had trapped beavers with pelts of this same silken texture and heft.

The next morning Tames Horses had struck his lodge and set off for this valley.

Less than an hour ago, his shrewd guess had resulted in a rifle ball in his shoulder. It had apparently not occurred to the mountain man that Tames Horses or any other Indian would know enough to realize this woman he had taken was Golden Hawk's sister. Apparently he was also unaware that Golden Hawk was searching for him.

Now it only remained for Tames Horses to live long enough to reach Fort Hall so he could tell his great friend Golden Hawk how to find this valley . . . and his sister.

About to enter the ravine where he had left his pony, Tames Horses pulled up, alert to trouble. Crouching, he entered the ravine. A great tawny shape lifted from his downed pony and glanced at him, its bloody, whiskered face alert, his great cat eyes glowing, then it bounded away and up the side of the ravine, vanishing in a shower of snow.

Tames Horses took this as a bad sign. It was his fault. If he had not tethered his pony in such a restricted spot, the mountain cat would not have found him such a tempting target. He carefully strapped to him what gear he could carry, left the ravine, and plowed through the waist-deep drifts as he continued up the slope, heading for the pass he had used earlier.

By now the valley was in shadow, giving his old eyes some relief from the snow's glare, but the night's chill would soon be coming on, and since he had decided he could not lug his small sleeping tent with him, he would have to find shelter for his night's camp. Shelter and rest. And soon. Already he felt a light-headedness coming on. He knew what that meant. He was losing blood steadily. For the first time it occurred to him that he might not make it back to Fort Hall, that Golden Hawk might never find this valley and his sister.

The thought galvanized him, and his gaze searched the rocky flanks of the slope above him, searching for the caves he knew were up there. After a moment or two, he spotted a cavern high above him, and started for it.

A long meadow fronted the steep, rocky flank where the cavern was located. Pushing through the deep snow, he pulled himself up the boulders beneath the cavern and finally stomped into its entrance. He was pleased to be putting the snow behind him, but as he moved deeper into the cavern, he became aware of the smell of bear. He glanced quickly around him and then up at the ceiling. It was at least thirty feet high. Farther in, a smaller cave ran off the main cavern. Exploring this cave cautiously, he found the animal smell too powerful for him. A primitive, root-deep alarm rang within him. He decided he would remain outside in the larger cavern for the night.

He was about to gather wood for a fire when he caught sight of a young male grizzly charging into the meadow, four timber wolves on his heels. Dangling from the bear's jaws was a newly killed badger, and it was this steaming, half-devoured morsel the wolves were after. Once in the meadow, the wolves circled the bear and closed in.

The grizzly, in a fury of exasperation, set two of the younger wolves spinning with a single, ferocious cuff of his paw, but when he tried to continue on across the meadow, the deep snow so hindered the bear that the two older wolves, backs arched, fangs clicking, shot toward him like twin gray lightning bolts.

With perfect teamwork, the two wolves passed on either side of him, the large male a second or two ahead of the female. As the male caught at the badger with his teeth, the force of his charge yanked the badger out of the grizzly's mouth just as the female snapped savagely at the bear's neck. With a furious roar, the bear swung away from her mate and tumbled backward into a drift, his four feet in the air.

At once the two younger wolves flashed forward to rip and tear at the bear's exposed belly. The bear rolled frantically as all four wolves attack him. Then, exploding with rage and fear, the bear rose to his full height and uttered a roar that shook the mountainside. He turned swiftly, and swept the air about him with his huge front paw. The awesome swipe caught one of the young wolves and sent it tumbling backward through the snow. Yelping like a chastized puppy, the wolf slunk off, its back laid open from shoulder to ham.

But this treatment of one of their family members only roused the other three wolves to greater fury and renewed determination. They darted in, struck at the bear's flanks, flashed out, spun around, and came at him from another direction, nipping and slashing as they raced past. It was a dizzying, devastating performance, and before long, the bear knew he was fighting for his life.

Absorbed in the battle below him, Tames Horses became aware that something vast and powerful was moving up on him from behind. Turning swiftly, he saw a huge male grizzly ambling toward him on his way out of the cavern. Reaching for his knife with his left hand, Tames Horses prepared to die for the second time that day. But as the grizzly got closer, he seemed not see the Indian. The great beast appeared unsteady, and at once Tames Horses realized the animal had just been roused from his winter sleep and was still groggy and not at all happy at being awakened.

Tames Horses ducked swiftly back off the cavern's apron into a rocky niche to get out of the bear's way. The great-grandfather of all grizzlies moved past him. The sounds of the stuggle below in the snow came sharply now, the young grizzly roaring and snapping as he whirled frantically about to keep his attackers at bay. Drawn to the edge of the cavern, the enormous grizzly rose up on his hind legs, peering with mean, red-eyed anger at the contest below him. Once the significance of the uneven battle filtered into his sleep-fogged brain, the big grizzly uttered a deep, surly roar, slammed down onto all fours, and loped from the cavern, plowing down through the snow to join the young grizzly in battle.

With awesome power, the huge male lay about him with his fearsome claws. The scalp of the male wolf was peeled back, and the second youngster limped off, yelping piteously and dragging a shattered hind leg after it.

The battle was over.

But even as the mother wolf flashed after her retreating family, she snatched out of the snow the remains of the badger.

Both grizzlies now rose on their hind legs and stared at each other, the large male towering over the younger bear. Not a sound was uttered by either animal. But the smaller bear came down soundlessly onto his forepaws, turned, and ambled swiftly back across the field to disappear into a line of trees. The big grizzly dropped to his four feet then and hustled back up the slope to the cavern and his interrupted slumber.

Tames Horses froze as the giant bear paused at the cavern entrance and raised his nose to sniff the air. Troubled, the bear rose onto his hind legs, his front paws hanging loosely, his sensitive nose twitching. Tames Horses tightened his grip on his knife. With a sound that was more like a bark than a growl, the bear dropped onto his front paws and disappeared into the cavern.

There was no question now of Tames Horses staying in this cavern. As soon as he lit his fire, he would have a visitor—an unhappy, irritable, large visitor who was anxious to get back to sleep. Reluctantly, Tames Horses left the protection of the cavern and headed toward the stream he had glimpsed earlier.

Along the stream bank he found shelter inside a dense tangle of berry vines and mountain laurel over which the snow had formed a solid roof. Using his knife, he cut several evergreen boughs and piled them on the frozen snow inside the shelter. Then he went back to the site of the battle he had just witnessed and searched until he cut the trail the fleeing wolves had left.

Following their spoor through a patch of trees, he came to a frozen stream, crossed it, and came upon the body of the young wolf the first grizzly had ripped open. The wolf was already cold, but not yet stiff, and its body was stretched out as far as it could go, as if the wolf were still trying to catch up with the others. Straddling the still form, Tames Horses rolled the wolf over onto its back, then plunged his knife deep into the animal's chest and ripped it down the length of the carcass all the way into the crotch. Then, reaching into the steaming entrails, he pulled forth the animal's liver, sliced it quickly if clumsily with his left hand, and devoured it raw. He felt a lift almost at once.

He took the wolf by the tail, slung it over his shoulder, and started back to his shelter. It was almost dark when he got there, but there remained enough light in the sky for him to find dry firewood. He built a fire on a floor of logs, fashioned a spit, and later, with the moon rising over his shoulder, dined on roasted wolf meat. Afterward, he sliced the palatable meat that was left into strips and hung them on frozen vines to jerk them. He would need this meat for the journey ahead of him. He could not rely on the Animal That Walks Like a Man to continue to provide for his needs.

But already Tames Horses was impressed. The signs were good. His medicine was powerful. It had sent those two bears to provide him with what he would need for his journey. Even the ache in his right shoulder was fading somewhat.

At last, his campfire flickering low, his belly full, Tames Horses crawled in under his roof of snow and lay down on the evergreen boughs. Taking out his knife, he clasped it firmly in front of his face and was soon asleep.

A week later, Cal Banyan, on his way to Fort Hall with a wagon full of freight, pulled back on his reins and laid aside his bullwhip. A bent, yet sturdy old Indian had appeared out of a snowbank beside the trail. He was holding his right arm stiffly, and was wrapped in a ragged Hudson's Bay blanket.

As Banyan reached for his rifle, the Indian held up his hand in the traditional sign for peace. Banyan relaxed. This old prune of an Indian was nothin' to be afeared of; hell, he didn't even have a hoss. Nothin' more pitiful than a redskin without a hoss.

"You waitin' for spring?" Banyan called.

"No," replied the Indian with great dignity. "Wait for you. See you come from mountain. Where you go?"

"Fort Hall."

"That is what I think."

"You want a ride?"

The Indian nodded and climbed carefully onto the seat beside Banyan, using only his left hand. He seemed to be in some pain, and as Banyan looked closely at the old Indian's face, he noticed how pale it looked and how washed out were his eyes. It dawned on him then that the Indian had been wounded in some fashion, not that the old warrior would let on, of course.

Banyan shrugged. He knew it would be useless to ask the Indian what the hell he was doing standing out there in the snow. But he was glad for the company, and without further conversation he sent a dark arrow of tobacco juice into a snowbank to his left, cracked the whip over the backs of his mules, and started up.

The next time he glanced over, he saw that the Indian was leaning back against the canvas, eyes closed, apparently unconscious. Frowning, Banyan slapped the reins over the mules' backs to get more speed out of them.

This Indian wasn't going to be much company, after all.

— 10 —

After shooting the Indian and knocking Annabelle unconscious, Gar was still beside himself when he reached the cabin. Dumping Annabelle brutally on the hard-packed dirt floor of the cabin, he snatched up a piece of firewood and proceeded to beat her mercilessly about the head and shoulders.

After a nightmarish, indeterminate time, she roused herself and set to work about the cabin, her head aching with a steady constancy that did not leave her night or day, staying with her even into her nightmares. In addition, she had an odd sense of unreality, and was unable to focus her eyes. Handling the most ordinary chores seemed close to impossible. Reaching for dishes, she missed. About the fireplace she dropped pots and pans, seemingly unable to concentrate for long on any chore. She had to plan carefully the execution of such simple tasks as setting the table.

When it became obvious that she was unable to function, a curiously chastened Gar led her back to her bed and saw to it that she stayed there. In the weeks and months that followed, she was too incoherent to eat and lost weight rapidly until she did not herself know how she was managing to stay alive. But stay alive she did with a tenacity that wrung a grudging respect from Gar, along with a surprising remorse, something he had never felt before in his life. He found it be an unsettling emotion.

At last the ceaseless pounding in her head faded, the nightmares came no more, and one morning she awoke to see sunlight streaming in through the window of her room and realized that she did not have to struggle to focus her eyes, that she was finally on the mend. Gar, whom she realized with some wonder had nursed her through her convalescence, made no demands upon her and saw to it that the fire in the fireplace would last during the periods when he was gone. When she was able to sit up, he fed her meat broths that required some trouble in their preparation, and while the winter winds howled and stomped about the little cabin, he saw to it that she was kept warm and fed and safe.

For her part, Annabelle said nothing to remind Gar that it was he who had struck her down in the first place. Still bedridden, she stared about her at the rough-hewn walls of her tiny bedroom, and aware of her fragile, sticklike figure and sunken cheeks, she realized his blows had caused a concussion, perhaps even worse. She had seen men kicked by horses back East who staggered about as she had.

Now that he had no reason to punish her in order to compel obedience, Gar seemed almost gentle. More than once Annabelle caught him peering at her in an odd way, as if, perplexed, he were trying to place her in a different, earlier time and was struggling to recall it.

Suddenly it was spring. A warm April sun was shrinking the snow fields on all sides of the cabin and patches of dark, wet ground were showing through. The pine branches were no longer freighted with snow. Soon she was on her feet again, capable of light work like cleaning the cabin and preparing meals, all of which she did automatically, out of a sense of obligation for the care Gar had given her during her long recuperation.

One evening, after his return from a trap-setting trip, she tried to talk to him, to find out something of the strange, solitary white hunter's past life. Only in this way, she felt, could she communicate with the man on a decent, human level.

"Did you come from the East, Mr. Trimm?" she asked as she set the table. During his absence, in order to keep her mind off her miserable plight, she had cut an empty flour sack into squares and sewed them together to fashion a tablecloth. She was not surprised that he did not notice it as he sat down to the table.

"Came from St. Louis," he told her, glancing back at the stove where the elk steaks and potatoes were cooking.

She finished setting the table and then brought the food over on two large plates she used for platters. As she sat down, she glanced at him and watched him fill his plate.

"St. Louis? That's a lovely city. I went through there a few months ago on my way out here." Even as she spoke, the enormity of what had befallen her since that journey began almost caused her to choke up.

"What's that? Lovely city, did ye say?"

She nodded, filling her plate, guardedly optimistic that she had finally managed to start a conversation with this huge animal of a man. "Yes," she repeated, "I found it a lovely city, so modern and bustling."

"Not the part I knowed," he said, shoveling the food into the hole in his hairy face, his eyes regarding her with cold interest.

"Oh."

"What I remembers is mud and cold and pigs and cockroaches. The place stank."

"Yes," she agreed, sorry now that she had hit upon this topic. "I suppose there are parts of St. Louis that are distinctly unpleasant."

"I have nightmares," he admitted through chomps, "about St. Louis. I hate the place. Won't never go there agin, less'n I go to hell."

"I see."

They ate in silence for a long while, then she looked up at him and cleared her throat. "I'm grateful to you, Mr. Trimm," she told him, "for taking care of me this past winter, but you must understand that I am a married woman, that I belong to another man."

He stared at her for a long moment with his black, sullen eyes. "You're my woman now, and make no mistake about it."

"But my husband is a very famous man. He has come all the way from Washington to map out a new route to Oregon."

"That so?"

"Yes."

His eyebrows canted slightly and she thought he might be smiling. "And yer brother is Golden Hawk. I saw you with him at Fort Hall."

"And that means nothing to you, Mr. Trimm?"

"No, it don't. I take what I want in this world. And this valley is my world. So let's hear no more about it.

You're my woman now. Best get used to it. And bring me some coffee before it boils away."

She got up and hurried to the stove. From his tone Annabelle knew enough not to press the issue any further. Gar had instilled in her a great respect for his rages. No Indian, no matter how furious he might have been, had ever beaten her with such terrible ferocity. Deep inside Gar Trimm a gear had slipped at that moment, and he had become no longer responsible for his actions.

She dared not duplicate the circumstances.

That night, in her small bedroom, Gar asserted his claim. Still weak, she was no match for him. Her resistance collapsed after a short struggle. Gar did not even seem to notice that she had tried to deny him. He took what he wanted with quick, brutal efficiency.

Two days later, with much of the snow gone from the fields, they left the cabin and moved deeper into the valley. To Annabelle's astonishment, Gar burned the cabin to the ground after taking from it whatever essentials they would need. She realized then that he was doing this as a precaution to make sure no more Indians or white men stumbled upon them. She sensed also that it was a move he took for deeper, more primitive reasons. He was retreating farther from civilization, thereby strengthening his hold over the woman he had taken.

What he did not fully realize was that Annabelle was a woman who was at least as comfortable in the wilderness as she had ever been in an upholstered parlor in Cambridge, Massachusetts.

Gar seemed to know precisely where he was going, and Annabelle realized he must have scouted out his destination during his long, earlier absences from the cabin. After clamboring over melting snows and across swollen streams, they climbed an almost sheer face of rock to a cave high above the valley floor. The cave's entrance was screened by the tops of the towering pines that grew from the slopes below. The ledge leading into the cave's mouth was inaccessible except on foot. The horses Gar left below to graze in the meadow near the cliff face.

Set into the valley's west wall, the cave was warmed by the morning sun, and free of prevailing winds. A hollow in the shelf at the cave's entrance made a good place for a cooking fire. Layers of hides over pine boughs created comfortable beds inside. This, then, would be the new home of Gar Trimm and his recently taken bride.

In the weeks that followed, Annabelle made no more attempts to engage the huge mountain man in intelligent conversation or to inquire about his past. Instead, she kept herself scrupulously busy and did as she was told without comment, retreating carefully, deeply into herself so that an essential part of her became untouched, pristine.

On the nights when he claimed her, she did not resist, and Gar did not notice, afterward, her furious, silent tears. He did not notice, either, how quiet and independent she was becoming. She was not in awe of the wilderness or of the forest animals, including the huge bears. She allowed herself to feast on the majestic peaks rimming the valley and to gaze down in wonder at the steep-sided chasms and the roaring rapids that seemed to fill every ravine and hollow as spring blanketed the world with sunshine and new, fresh color. When Gar was off setting his traps in the evening or leaving before dawn to harvest his pelts, or when he was hunting game, she took the opportunity to explore the valley about the cave. Never, however, did she allow herself to go so far as to be unable to return before Gar.

She had no desire for him to know how much of her prison was becoming familiar to her.

She would never know for how long at a time Gar would be gone. But she realized that on each expedition, he stayed longer and then it occurred to her why this was so. As the trapping season progressed, Gar was trapping more and more distant streams. When she caught in the evening sky a thin line of smoke lifting from a campfire on the other side of a distant pass, she decided it was time for her to make her move.

The next morning, as soon as Gar vanished into the timber below the cave, she snatched up the blanket roll she had cached weeks before in a rocky cranny deep in the cave, and left. Inside the blanket she carried a side of salted deer meat and a skinning knife with a broken handle that Gar had let her use. It was not much, but she was hoping it would be enough to get her to the Indians or trappers who had lit the campfire the evening before.

She was through the pass by midmorning, heading down the eastern slope of the mountain range, but after that, her sense of direction seemed to desert her. One trail led her into an impassable canyon, another brought her to the brink of a chasm she could not cross. For a moment she thought almost longingly of the cave; then, in a fury at herself for such weakness, she turned away from the chasm and pushed on to the east until she found herself once again moving downslope. Abruptly, she came to the edge of a pine-studded ridge and beheld a staggering vista.

The whole of the eastern slopes of the Rocky Mountains seemed to open out before her. She was astonished and intimidated by the enormous range that stretched hundreds of miles to the east, south, and north. Layer and layer of soaring peaks and dark-green forests met her gaze. How could she ever find her way through all that wilderness?

Well, she couldn't, she realized—not alone.

Something caught her eye. She squinted and shaded her eyes, since her bonnet had long since fallen away to tatters. There it was, far off to the southeast, a thread of smoke reaching upward until it vanished into the bright-blue sky.

Smoke. Smoke from a campfire. Was this the same party that had built its fire the night before? she wondered. And were these white trappers or Indians? And then she realized it did not matter. No Indian or white man could be more terrible a punishment for a white woman than Gar Trimm. She would take her chances on the devil she did not know. The one she did know was terrible enough.

She moved off the ridge and set her direction toward the smoke she glimpsed only fitfully in the hours ahead and then not at all during the afternoon. When night came she found shelter under some low pines and wrapped herself in her blankets against the inevitable cold that came with each night in the high country. As soon as she rested her cheek on her arm, she slept.

She awoke with the sky blue overhead, the pine branches dripping dew onto her face and neck. After taking care of her meager toilet, she sliced a chunk of the meat and ate it as ravenously as any wild animal. Then she continued on down the long meadow she had camped above, heading in what she hoped was the correct direction, for this time there was no beckoning finger of smoke to guide her steps.

Once she reached the grassy meadows and the wooded slopes of the foothills, she found herself hopelessly lost. There were no clear paths to follow, only confusing and numerous game trails that tempted her first this way and then that. She decided her best course would be to let herself be guided by one of the many streams that were surging down out of the mountains. She found one that appeared docile enough for her to follow and managed to keep alongside it through a low pass that took her into another open park.

She started across it and was in the middle of it when she caught sight of the grizzly. She had seen plenty of grizzlies in the valley, but always from a good distance. She expected them to turn and run from her as soon as they saw her or caught her scent, and they always did.

This one didn't.

It saw her at precisely the same time she saw it and lifted up onto its hind legs and stared at her with great curiosity. It was enormous. Her heart thudding in her chest, Annabelle saw the grizzly drop onto all fours and start across the open meadow toward her.

Annabelle knew that if she ran, the bear would run also. It would be a normal response to a creature running before it. She decided to resume walking at a normal pace and started up. The bear ambled after her, unhurried, and Annabelle relaxed some. She knew she was doing the right thing. In a few minutes the bear would lose interest in her and amble off after a butterfly.

She hoped.

Abruptly the bear increased its pace, seemingly determined to get a much closer look at the curious two-legged creature in the ragged dress. And then Annabelle realized what was drawing the bear after her—the meat she was carrying! But it was all she had. She did not want the bear to have it. She would starve!

Foolishly, she started to run. At once the bear put its head down and increased its speed. Realizing her error, Annabelle tried frantically to unwrap the chunk of meat while still running full-tilt. A second before reaching the edge of a wooded slope, she managed to separate the meat from the blanket and fling it to the ground behind her. A single, terrified glance back showed the enormous beast was almost upon her and still running full tilt, the meat lying on the ground just ahead of it. And there was no assurance whatsover in the bear's manner that this single piece of meat would be enough to satisfy it.

And then she was crashing down the slope, floundering blindly, her only thought to distance herself from the bear. Branches raked her arms and face as she blundered through the pines. The slope was so steep, her legs were soon aching. Blood pounded in her ears. She slipped on pine needles and went sprawling. Scrambling back up on her feet, she dared another look back, caught a glimpse of gray at the edge of the trees above her, and plunged on.

An opening appeared in the trees below her. She stumbled toward it and found herself on a well-worn game trail and plunged on. Someone rose from the brush beside the trail and stepped in front of her. A mountain man, not an Indian. In the instant she caught sight of him, she thought he was faintly familiar. With a scream of surprise, then gratitude, she flung herself toward him, then collapsed, sobbing, into his arms.

"Hey, now," the mountain man said, in a rough but gentle voice, "didn't mean to give you such a scare."

"A grizzly!" she cried. "It's chasing me."

"No, it ain't, ma'am. It's eatin' that meat you done dropped in front of it. Right smart thinkin' that was."

She glanced back up the slope to see if he was right. The trail was empty. The huge bear had taken her bait. With a deep, trembling sigh she allowed herself to stand back from the man, feeling immediately ashamed at her previous lack of composure. She had never been that frightened in her life, but it was no excuse, she told herself. "I've seen you before," she said.

"Yes, ma'am, you have. At Fort Hall. Name's Hal Clampert. Old Bill Williams introduced us."

"I remember, yes."

"You been gone a long time, I hear."

"The absence was not of my choosing, Mr. Clampert."

"Call me Hal, ma'am. Yep, we all knowed you was carried off by a Comanche war party that got inside the fort. Then we heard other things—mighty peculiar things. About Gar Trimm."

"That wild man took me from three Blackfoot, killed them all, then abducted me. I was fleeing from him as much as from that grizzly when you saw me."

"You ain't got to worry none now," Clampert

assured her. "You're safe. I'll take you back to Fort Hall. Hawk will sure be glad to see you."

"And what of my husband? Is he there now?"

"Gone to Californy with a scouting expedition. Joe Meek is their scout, so he'll be back before long."

Annabelle took a sudden deep breath. She had escaped Gar Trimm and would soon be on her way back to the fort. For a moment she could hardly believe her good fortune. But when she considered a moment and realized how wild Gar would be when he found her gone, she realized her good fortune rested on a very thin reed. Hal Clampert was no match for the likes of Gar Trimm. If Gar overtook them, it would mean death for Clampert and worse for her.

"I should warn you," she told Clampert. "I am sure Gar is close behind me. When he returned last night, he must have discovered that I'd fled and is probably after me now."

"I know Gar. A tough man. A loner. Like a grizzly bear. A good woodsman and a fine hunter and trapper. Some say he could track a butterfly over water. Guess we better cover our tracks."

"Do you have horses?"

"Yes, back down the slope. Follow me."

Clampert was a big man in his late fifties, she guessed, with snowy white hair that reached clear to his shoulders and a thick, yellowing handlebar mustache. His eyes were hazel and kindly, and he seemed genuinely glad to have found Annabelle. As they walked, he explained how he happened to be in those bushes waiting for her.

He had seen Annabelle from a considerable distance, just as he topped a ridge and pulled his horse to a halt to let it blow. When he saw her disappear into the gorge, he left the ridge and rode hard to intercept her. He was cutting up the slope toward her when he saw the bear chasing her. He saw her throw the piece of meat to the ground and continue her flight, plunging blindly down the slope toward him. He had his rifle ready in case the grizzly followed her. When the bear came to a shambling halt over the meat, he put his rifle away and waited for her to get to him.

"You didn't waste no time a'tall gettin down that slope," he finished up, chuckling.

"I had incentive," Annabelle agreed, smiling for the first time in a long time.

Clampert gave Annabelle his saddled horse and gallantly repacked his packhorse and rode that, even though he had no saddle. Cautious, for Clampert knew as well as Annabelle what kind of man they were dealing with, he kept to the stream bed of the stream Annabelle had followed through the gorge and stayed with it until they could leave it deep in the timber, where the resilient pine needles left no trace of their horses' hooves. Late in the afternoon they entered a deep valley through which another stream flowed, this one south. As they rode on, Annabelle noted that while the cold shadows of night were already enclosing them, the high peaks above remained bathed in full daylight. They kept to the gravelly stream bed again and kept going until close to midnight before making camp.

Thoroughly exhausted by this time, Annabelle ate little and rolled almost at once into her blanket, while Clampert took out his pipe and sat down beside the low campfire for a last smoke, he told her, before retiring for the night. Earlier, he had assured her they had done a good job of throwing Gar off her trail. He had insisted she shouldn't worry, that the important thing for her now was to relax and get a good night's sleep. They had a long ride still ahead of them.

It was just what Annabelle wanted to hear. She watched Clampert puffing on his clay pipe and felt a strong welling of gratitude toward this unassuming trapper. But before she could find any words adequate to express her emotion, or decide if the words would simply embarrass him, she slept.

The rage he had felt when he returned to the cave to find Annabelle gone still seethed within Gar as he crawled across a shoulder of smooth rock and surveyed the campsite below him.

He had caught sight of the two riders late that afternoon. The care the man with her took to cover their tracks had been futile. Gar had come upon the grizzly not long after it had gorged itself on the meat Annabelle had flung before it. And once Gar saw how the man tried to hide his tracks by riding along the stream bed, he knew he was dealing with a fool and realized he would have no difficulty overtaking them both.

He had left his horse farther back. It was unshod, but a hoof could still sound clearly on rock, and he wanted to make his rush with complete surprise. Moving like a great lizard across the rocks, Gar started down the slope. The sound of the water rushing past the campsite covered the sound of Gar's approach nicely. When he reached the edge of the clearing where they were camped, he saw the man was still awake, his features showing clearly in the campfire's dancing light. He was smoking a clay pipe, short, contented puffs coming from his mouth. Watching him, Gar felt cold rage knotting his belly.

Then, looking closer, Gar realized he knew the man. It was Hal Clampert, a fur trapper like himself. He had come out here a little after General Ashley had and, like Gar, never had a partner, though at one time it was rumored he had become partial to Flathead women. Clampert was too old for that now. And the damn fool sure as hell wasn't going to get any older.

Gar inched forward. He carried four weapons: his Hawken rifle, primed and loaded; his horse pistol, also ready to fire; his skinning knife in its sheath; and his small shingling hatchet. This last weapon was an all-purpose tool used for everything from scraping hides to hammering stakes to breaking bones for cooking. It was a formidable weapon, and in hand-to-hand fighting, he preferred it.

Clampert was less than thirty feet away. Beside him on the grass was his long Kentucky rifle, and Gar had no doubt it was all primed and ready to fire. Slowly gathering himself for the attack, Gar let his anger out of his body, allowing it to pound in his brain. Then he eased from his prone position until he was in a low crouch. He shifted his rifle into his left hand and tugged his short hatchet from its slot in his belt, hefting it in his right hand.

He attacked silently. There was almost no warning until he was there, his small ax raised, ready to strike. Even so Clampert heard the whisper of danger and tried to evade it. His small pipe dropping from his mouth, he rose, turning, just as Gar brought the heavy, sharp-edged hatchet down in a chopping stroke. Instead of crushing the man's spine as Gar had intended, the ax's honed edge sliced into the white trapper's back.

He screamed and toppled forward, bowled off his feet by the force of the blow.

Behind Gar, Annabelle cried out. He swung around at her cry and saw her sitting bolt upright in her blanket, staring at him in horror.

He turned back to Clampert. The hatchet buried in his back twisting his face into a mask of agony, the trapper had managed to seize his rifle and was trying to bring it up to sight on Gar's back. Gar saw the long barrel lifting toward him. He didn't hesitate. He fired his rifle and saw Clampert's body jerk from the impact.

Behind Gar rose a terrified sobbing, almost a whimper. Annabelle. She had betrayed him, gone off with this white trapper willingly. And now she was seeing how he made that man pay for taking her. But it was for this stinking white trapper that she cried out. The knowledge of this added fuel to his killing rage. Without a glance back at Annabelle, he bent close over Clampert. The trapper was still alive, the bullet having left a leaking hole inches above his belly button. Gar unsheathed his knife and with a few deft movements of the blade, circled the top of Clampert's head. He grabbed the still-living man's graying hair in his left hand and snapped sharply, lifting the scalp from Clampert's skull. Then he stood back and calmly kicked the trapper in the side of the head, sending him rolling over onto his back. Clampert's eyes flickered dully, painfully.

"You ain't dead yet," Gar snarled down at the prostrate body, "but by the time the buzzards come to pick your bones clean, you'll be wishin' you was."

From behind him, he heard Annabelle racing frantically off through the brush. He turned and loped easily after her, catching her from behind with little difficulty. As she tried to fight him off, he clenched his fist and struck her as hard as he could on the side of her face, careful this time to do no injury to her head. The blow was enough to take the fight out of her and she collapsed, sobbing weakly, on the ground at his feet.

He stood over her, filled with his triumph. She had run off, but he had come after her, killed the one who took her, and punished her good and proper. Now that he thought of it, this was probably a good thing.

"You see what you done?" he taunted her. "You best remember this. Won't do you no good to run off on me. I'll always be comin' after you."

Without waiting for dawn, Gar planted Annabelle in the saddle of the hunter's horse, then pointed his own mount northeast toward his hidden valley. Annabelle, her face swollen and discolored from Gar's single, vicious blow, rode behind, her quiet sobs lost in the sound of their passage over the dark ground.

— 11 —

Hawk shot bolt upright in his sleeping blanket. "What's that?" he barked.

Beside him, Brad Balfour came awake more slowly, muttering and scratching his head. "I didn't hear a thing," he said.

But Tames Horses was already on his feet, his rifle in his hand, peering off to the northeast. The old Indian had heard it too, Hawk realized. A shot. A single rifle shot, its sound carried far by the echoing mountain walls that enclosed them. Hawk looked up at the moonless sky. Judging from the inclination of the Big Dipper, he knew it to be a little after midnight.

A rifle shot this time of night did not indicate a man hunting game—except in self-defense. And that wasn't likely. At this hour, a single gunshot meant ambush . . or murder.

Throwing off his blanket, Hawk got to his feet and walked over to Tames Horses, moving as softly as possible in order not to miss the report of more shots. Without a word Tames Horses pointed in the direction from which the shot had come. There was no need for either man to say anything as they listened, heads

151

lifted slightly. But no more shots came. After waiting about five minutes, the two men got back into their sleeping blankets.

Before long the sound of Tames Horses' steady breathing joined that of Brad Balfour's. But Hawk could not sleep. He folded his arms under his head and stared up at the stars, but he did not see them. He was thinking of Annabelle. Was she dead? Could that distant, echoing shot have had anything to do with her or her captor, Gar Trimm? Of course it was highly unlikely, but the way the sound had knifed through his sleep gave Hawk pause. It was as if, at the same moment he had heard the shot, he had heard Annabelle scream.

He shuddered at the thought and then realized ruefully that he was not helping himself by going on like this.

After recovering from his lance wound under Ana Dolores' care, Hawk had gone south with Old Bill and René on the chance that Gar Trimm might have circled south into the mountains of New Mexico to avoid the winter . . . and pursuit. Old Bill knew that Gar used to trap around Bent's Fort until the beaver gave out in the mountains west and north of it, and so the three men spent considerable time at the fort and in the mountains nearby, asking about Gar. Then René left to return to New Orleans, and Old Bill, ignoring everyone's advice, sold his wife to a lonely trapper and went back to his Ute Indians. The Ute had become a bold and troublesome tribe of late.

Early in April Hawk left Bent's Fort and drifted north in time for a late chinook. As he neared Fort Hall, the snow appeared to vanish before his eyes as the chinook's unnaturally hot winds ate up the last vestiges of winter. When he reached Fort Hall, he found that Tames Horses had arrived at the fort shortly after Hawk had left.

The old Indian had staggered from Cal Banyan's wagon more dead than alive. Though Dr. Phineas P. Burke was on hand to offer his bleeding pan, Walsh kept him away from the old warrior and did not interfere when Tames Horses was taken in by an old Shoshone crone who had been doing a fine business outside the fort's walls selling medicine bags to would-be warriors. Indeed, so successful had some of those warriors become that she was becoming famous. Whatever it was, magic or good medicine, she pulled Tames Horses through the winter and he was among the first to greet Hawk on his return from Bent's Fort. He wasted no time telling Hawk of Gar Trimm's hidden valley.

As a result of the snakebite, Brad Balfour now walked with a slight limp but as everyone told him to be, he was grateful that this was his only permanent reminder of his encounter with the Comanche and Blackfoot warriors. After all, he still had his scalp.

However, Balfour seemed to have learned little from the experience. He would still go on at foolish lengths about the life-styles and customs of the "noble red men" who came and went from the fort and seemed incapable of understanding the true nature of the great wilderness that stretched along the spine of the continent. But if his childlike innocence was exasperating to those around him, especially the mountain men, it was also somewhat touching. He was like a naïve child walking amid yawning crocodiles, commenting on their lovely smiles.

Though Hawk had tried to dissuade Balfour from

accompanying him and Tames Horses, the young man had insisted, and in the end Hawk had capitulated, his impatience giving away finally to an awareness of Balfour's profound and genuine concern for Annabelle. If the man wanted to accompany them, he did not see that he had the right to stop him.

Meanwhile, the one troubling question that nagged Hawk was whether or not Gar had fled the valley after Tames Horses approached him. It was with this last question still plaguing him that Hawk closed his eyes wearily and sank into a troubled sleep.

The next morning they came upon the dead trapper, Clampert, and knew that it was indeed a murder they had heard take place the night before.

After examining the dead man, noting the ax wound in his back and the neat scalping job, Hawk moved back and shook his head ruefully.

"My God," Balfour breathed, his eyes wide with shock, "who do you think did this?"

"Could have been a lone Blackfoot on a raid to gain a scalp and some renown. I don't think it was more than one."

"But we're not in Blackfoot country, are we?"

"We're close enough. Besides, Blackfoot country is wherever a Blackfoot warrior steps."

Hawk looked up at the bright morning sky. Buzzards were already coasting in long circles overhead, like giant cinders caught in an updraft. They had no shovel to dig a grave and the ground was still too frozen for digging anyway. Clampert would have to provide nourishment for buzzards, it appeared.

Hawk was turning back to his horse when Tames Horses came over and handed him a few strands of hair, gossamer threads that shone like spun gold. Taking the hair from the Indian, Hawk felt his heart skip a beat. Then he looked back down at the sprawled, scalped hunter and realized his attacker had not been a single Blackfoot warrior out for glory, but Gar Trimm taking back his woman captive. Annabelle had tried to escape with Clampert's help and Gar had come after them, killing Clampert for his trouble. He had heard Annabelle scream, after all.

He swung onto his horse grimly. All they had to do now was follow the tracks left by Gar's mounts and then take the son of a bitch.

But they lost Gar's tracks soon after they started. Fortunately, they kept on, and Tames Horses had no difficulty finding the valley. Two days later the three men, their horses tethered in a hidden grove behind them, filtered cautiously through the timber toward the cabin Tames Horses promised was just ahead.

But when Hawk broke out into the clearing, his heart sank. All that was left of the cabin was a blackened crater, its fieldstone fireplace and chimney a lonely marker. Gar had indeed lit out after his encounter with Tames Horses and with discouraging thoroughness had burned his bridges behind him.

Where had Gar gone? Had he kept to the valley or had he found another hiding place outside it? There were countless peaks, valleys, and hidden ravines in this vaulting wilderness. How were they to find him after this?

"Now, what?" Balfour asked bleakly, coming over to stand beside Hawk.

"Gar's around here somewhere," Hawk muttered grimly.

"Yes, but where?"

155

Hawk saw Balfour gaze about him at the steep, heavily wooded slopes and the distant, snow-covered peaks beyond that hemmed them in. It was as if he were realizing for the first time the awesome dimensions of this country.

Tames Horses approached, his wrinkled face alert. He was not discouraged.

"What do you think, Tames Horses?" Hawk asked.

"Gar close by, I think."

"Still in this valley? He could be anywhere outside it."

The old Indian's black cherry eyes narrowed in speculation. "He tell me this valley is his. He hunt here many years. It is the beaver in this valley that make him rich. Gar not leave this valley. He still here somewhere."

Hawk liked the old man's reasoning and could find no hole in it. But where in this valley was Gar? And if he were still here, they had to be careful not to blunder onto him, allowing him enough time to use Annabelle as a shield. Hell, if he saw they had him cornered, he might kill her in a fit of rage. From what Hawk had learned of Gar at Bent's Fort, the lone mountain man was capable of any barbarity.

"If he's here, then," said Balfour, "how do we find him?"

"Split up," Hawk said. "You and Tames Horses circle the lake. I'll take the slopes."

"Better if we three split up," said Tames Horses. "We cover more ground quicker that way."

Hawk did not like the idea of Balfour stomping off through the wilderness on his own. Still, he had to go untethered one of these days, and this looked like the time for it. "All right, then. Balfour, I want you to be careful."

"Don't worry about me," Brad said, hefting his Remington rifle.

"Tames Horses, you take the area around the lake," Hawk said. "I'll take the far slopes, and Balfour, you take the slopes on this side. We'll meet back here in two days at the latest."

Glancing up in some awe at the steep, timbered slopes, Brad nodded. "That should give us plenty of time," he said. But he didn't sound all that certain of it to Hawk.

"If any of us finds where Gar and Annabelle are holed up," Hawk cautioned, "we'd better not try anything. We'll meet back here to make plans so we can take this son of a bitch without endangering Annabelle."

"Makes good sense," Brad agreed.

Tames Horses nodded solemnly and started back for his horse. Hawk and Balfour followed.

As soon as Gar got back to the cave with Annabelle, he fashioned a rawhide leash, one end of which he attached to a rocky projection deep inside the cavern, the other to her right ankle. He tied it securely enough so that she could not pull it off, but not so tight as to halt the circulation in her leg. It was for Annabelle the final humiliation.

She hardly noticed it when Gar took her the next night, managing somehow to block out almost completely the brutal copulation of her master. She was sickeningly aware of his foul seed in her, but she had a cold, unwavering faith that nothing of him would or could ever take root inside her. Her loathing for Gar was now such that it animated every sense, every nerve, every single cell in her body. For him even to come near her was to make her so livid with fury and hatred that even he was gradually dismayed by it.

And when she glanced up at times and saw the bitter bafflement in his eyes, she felt only a wild, atavistic joy.

Gar had left her that morning to set his traps. It was the first time since he had brought her back that he had left her alone. But he need not worry that she would run off again. And if she cut the rawhide, Annabelle knew he would only tie her up again with a shorter length.

She was washing her tin dishes and cups in a large iron pot, doing her best without soap in the icy spring water Gar had brought up for her, when she happened to glance down from the cave's entrance. What she saw made her heart stop.

Riding across the meadow below, almost into the trees at the far side by this time, she saw a lone rider. His back was to her, but there was something oddly familiar about the awkward way he sat his horse—and in that instant she realized who it was.

Brad!

As he vanished into the timber, she raced farther out onto the lip of the cave to shout to him and bring him back. With cruel suddenness, her right foot was yanked out from under her and she crashed facedown on the rocky surface. Numbed by the fall, confused and disoriented until she recalled her tethering, she crawled back along her leash and sat up, listening with dull, hopeless anger as the tin cup she had been washing clattered faintly on its way down the cliff face, to drop into the trees at the base.

Then, slowly, despite her immediate disappointment

hope shone forth. If Brad was in the valley, then so was Jed! They had found the place! The old Indian must have brought them. They knew she was here!

She picked herself up, and walking carefully to the farthest length of the rawhide, she stared wistfully down at the meadow, her heart pounding with new hope.

The faint sound caused Balfour to pull his horse to a halt and glance back over his shoulder. He could not hear the sound any longer, but that didn't matter. Deer or grizzly bears hardly ever drank from tin cups, and if there was one sound a man got to know intimately on the trail, it was that one. What Brad had heard was unmistakable: the clatter of a tin cup falling over a rock face.

Dismounting, he tethered his horse and walked back through the pines. Before he reached the clearing, he halted. He didn't need to go any farther. Directly in his line of sight through an opening in the pines that shielded it almost entirely, he could see a steep, scarred wall of rock, and on top of it a cave. At the cave's entrance was Annabelle, only her head and shoulders visible from where Balfour was standing.

Amazed, he continued on through the pines, but even before he reached the meadow, Annabelle was no longer in sight. He had dropped too far below the pines. He halted again to get the situation straight in his mind. Annabelle had been looking in his direction, so she must have seen him. That cup had probably been her way of signaling to him, which meant Gar was not around, or else he would have heard the cup, too.

Annabelle was alone, then!

Brad knew they had all agreed to meet back at the burned-out cabin before making a move. But there was Annabelle. In plain sight. Alone. He knew he could reach the cavern quickly. He was sure of it. Wouldn't it be better to bring Annabelle with him back to the cabin? Then they could go after Gar without worrying about her safety.

Besides, it was Annabelle they had come after.

The overwhelming good sense of this decided Balfour. At the edge of the timber, he surveyed the rock face and looked for a game trail of some kind that could take him up to the cave. He didn't have far to look, since there was the trail Gar had been using. It was dark with slicked mud, tracing a clear path to the ledge leading onto the cavern's apron.

Grinning, Balfour broke from the pines.

Gar had not gone to the lake or the large stream feeding it. He had taken his traps only part of the way, had cached them, and was now on his way back to the cave. He did not trust Annabelle. He knew she was pretty well cowed, but he could not be sure she really understood how impossible it was for her to escape him. So he was testing her. If he returned to find her still in the cave, the rawhide not untied or cut through, he would know then that she had accepted her place here with him.

As he moved back up through the timbered slope to the cave, he shook his head in puzzlement. He hated the way she was acting. He wanted her to laugh, to look at him from those blue eyes of hers without glowering. And on his couch at night, he wanted her to respond. The worse Indian squaw showed more passion than she did. Despite his towering need, the act was becoming unpleasant for him.

He reached the clearing and, glancing up, saw a man in buckskins stepping along the ledge leading into the cave, a long rifle in his hand.

"I can't believe it," Annabelle said, stepping back out of Brad's embrace. She knew she sounded foolish, but she didn't care.

What did bother her was how she looked. She could see it was pretty bad, judging from the look on Brad's face.

"Are . . . you all right?" Brad faltered, his eyes filled with concern.

"Of course, Brad. Now that you're here! Are you alone?"

"No. Your brother's with me. And Tames Horses, a Nez Percé Indian. The one you told to get Jed."

"I remember! But Gar shot him. And he was so old."

"He's a tough old bird," Brad said, laughing.

Taking his knife from its sheath, he cut through her rawhide leash with a single, angry slash.

"How far away are Jed and Tames Horses?" she asked.

"Not far. I'll take you to them. We're to meet at the burned cabin."

"Then you're alone?"

"For now, yes." He patted his rifle. "Don't worry. Me and this here Remington will take care of you. I've been doing a lot of practicing this winter at the fort. You'd be amazed at what a marksman I've become."

"I'm sure you've learned a lot, Brad."

The warmth in her voice caused him to blush slightly.

"Well, anyway, the first thing is to get you out of here and back safe with Jed. Then we'll take the measure of this wild man." He handed her his knife. "Here, maybe you better cut the rest of that rawhide off your ankle. We'll be riding over rough ground and it might get tangled in a branch or something."

She took the knife, bent, and slipping the cool blade between her flesh and the rawhide, sliced through her tether. As the sweaty rawhide parted from her ankle, she stood up, thrilled. She was finally willing to believe that she was really free.

"Ready?" she asked.

He nodded. Her glance went past him. Balfour saw something flash in her eyes. Then she screamed.

Balfour whirled in time to see Gar sweeping into the cave with the speed of a thunderbolt, his ax in his hand, his face wild with fury. Brad had the presence of mind to knock Annabelle to one side before he swung up his rifle. But he never got the chance to fire it. Gar grabbed the long barrel and wrested the Remington from Balfour's grasp with a single, shoulder-wrenching tug. As the long rifle clattered to the cave floor, Gar buried his ax in Balfour's chest, grabbed his shirt front with both hands, and flung him bodily across the cave.

The ax spun away when Balfour hit the rock floor. He tried to get up. Turning his head, he saw Gar approaching, then felt the big man's hands lifting him and propelling him with incredible ease out of the mouth of the cave. He felt himself falling, twisting slowly. Then came the first brush of the topmost branches, after which he began to slam down through the trees like a loose rag doll. Only he was not made of sawdust, but flesh and bone and sinew, and each time he struck a branch, he cried out in muffled, astonished pain.

When he hit the ground, he lay where he fell, unconscious.

Balfour stirred and came awake. Every muscle, every bone, it seemed, had been battered by the pine branches, and when he coughed, there was blood. He struggled to push himself up off the ground and realized that two ribs at least had been smashed. It felt as if a part of the ax was still lodged in his chest. He could feel the looseness inside when he moved, like water sloshing in a pail.

But he rose and staggered across the meadow and into the pines where he had left his horse. It was still there. It took a while for him to get into the saddle, but once he did, he lay across the horse's neck, and talking to it, pleading to it almost, he got it to move out.

The burned-out cabin was about a day's journey away. Maybe he could make it. For Annabelle's sake.

Balfour had not been finished off by Gar because he was caught up in a furious pursuit of Annabelle; from the moment Brad thrust her to one side, she saw her opportunity and took it. Turning her back on the two struggling men, she ran from the cave. She was familiar with the ledge leading from it and took the path down to the clearing in record time, the sound of her heavy breathing serving only to give her impetus. Reaching the clearing, she darted across it and vanished into the woods beyond.

She thought she heard Brad crying out and halted. But his cries faded, and then she saw Gar through the trees, already halfway down to the clearing. Turning, she bolted on through the pines, looking for a place to hide, and caught sight of a narrow cleft in the side of a mountain, its entrance hidden by thick grapevines. Snatching up a branch, she wiped away the traces of her tracks. Then, stepping only on patches of pine needles, she darted up the slope and into the cleft. All this time she had been carrying a knife, the one Brad had given her to cut through the rawhide.

She hefted it, and gradually her heavy breathing subsided and she had time to wonder what Gar might have done to Brad. But this was too terrible a thing to contemplate, and she forced herself to think of something else.

Like Jed coming all this way for her!

A moment later Gar charged past, barely looking at the ground. Her cleverness in wiping away her tracks had been wasted. But that did not matter. Brad had said that Jed and the Indian were at the cabin. And she knew where that was. Let Gar follow her. She would lead him to Jed, and Gar Trimm would get what was coming to him.

An arm as thick as a tree trunk snaked through the vines. Annabelle gasped and tried to jump back as Gar's hand closed like a vise about her left wrist and yanked her cruelly out of the cleft. There was a smile on his face as he twisted her wrist and drew her closer.

He did not see the knife in Annabelle's right hand as it flashed up and buried itself in his belly, hilt deep. The man gasped and staggered back, the knife twisting out of Annabelle's hand as he did so. Gar reached down and pulled the knife free, glancing up at her like a hurt child.

Annabelle darted past him down the slope and into

the pines. She fell once, scrambled to her feet, and kept going. She looked back and to her horror saw Gar stumbling doggedly after her. Turning back around, she plunged on, doubling her pace.

But she felt with terrifying certainty that no matter how fast she ran, she could never outdistance him.

It was past noon the following day when Hawk heard a hoarse cry and the sound of hooves. Tames Horses had arrived at the cabin only a few hours before and they had been waiting impatiently for Brad Balfour to show up.

Turning, they both saw Balfour ride out of the trees at the edge of the clearing. Hawk knew at once Brad was hurt. He was riding slumped forward over the horse's neck. Hawk swore bitterly as he skirted the cabin's ruin and ran toward Balfour. The wounded man halted his horse, then slid slowly to the ground, revealing a blood-slicked saddle and saddle blanket.

By the time Hawk and Tames Horses got to him, Brad was on his back, coughing, a thin line of blood trickling from one corner of his mouth. The blood that had stained the saddle came from a deep gash in his chest.

Hawk knelt beside him. "Well, Brad, I guess you found Gar. What about Annabelle?"

"She's alive. I . . . saw her . . . cave . . . a white wall of rock."

"How far?"

"Back there . . ." Gasping in pain, Balfour lifted his arm and tried to point.

"I know that cave," Tames Horses said quickly. "Not far from here. Maybe one day."

Hawk looked back down at Balfour. "Will you be all right?"

"Forget me. I'm all . . . broke inside. Get Annabelle!"

With a curt nod to Balfour, Hawk looked at Tames Horses and the two men hurried for their horses.

Riding off a moment later, Hawk glanced back at Balfour. The man was on his side, hugging his knees. He was not moving and could have been asleep, but Hawk doubted it. As Brad's form vanished from sight behind the screening trees, Hawk reflected grimly that the young man had undoubtedly ignored Hawk's warning to make no contact with either Annabelle or Gar before returning to the cabin.

But Hawk had no heart for blaming the man. It was Balfour's concern for Annabelle that had caused him to disobey, Hawk was sure. What worried Hawk was that in his eagerness to help Annabelle, Balfour might have succeeded only in making her situation worse.

After tethering their horses a safe distance back, Hawk and Tames Horses moved cautiously to the edge of the clearing below the cave. From where they stood, they could not see the cave. The tall pines on the white rock face hid its entrance completely. Slowly, they circled the meadow, keeping in the pines ringing it.

Then Hawk stopped, eyes wide, a tremor of blazing anger passing through him. Annabelle, bound in what appeared to be rawhide strips, was hanging from the cave's entrance by a single reata. She was not dead, and he could see her faint movements, like those of a struggling insect. The reata was looped around her chest and her hands were trussed behind her.

But her position was precarious. It would not take much to kill her. Gar had left her in plain sight as a lure to bring Hawk on the run, to make him expose himself. Somewhere on the lower lip of that cave, Gar was probably lying prone wih a rifle at his cheek, waiting for Hawk to break from cover.

Hawk studied the long trail that led up to the cave. It was obviously the route Gar used. But it was in plain sight from the cave above. Anyone charging up that trail would be a dead man before he got halfway up the cliffside.

Hawk glanced at Tames Horse. "I'm going around. I'll come down from above. When you see me on that ledge, start firing into the cave—and keep firing until I get inside."

"Then I go up trail."

Hawk nodded and handed Tames Horses his rifle, powder horn, and his sack of shot. Then he hurried back through the pines. Once out of sight of the cave, he made for the cliffside and started up the slope.

Clinging to small bushes, slipping on shale, and snatching at sharp, projecting rocks to keep himself from falling back, he lacerated his palms, which were soon slippery with blood. But he kept on doggedly until he was able to pull himself up onto the ridge above the rocky outcropping. As silently as a big cat, he moved along it until he was able to drop onto the ledge leading into the cave.

He dropped lightly to the ledge, grateful that he dislodged no stones or pebbles, the sound of which would have alerted Gar inside the cave. He paused to wipe his bloody palms off on the sides of his buckskins. Then he unsheathed his bowie and glanced down. Tames Horses was out of sight in the pines, but sud-

denly a rifle cracked, the sound of its round ricochet-
ing throughout the cavern. Almost without pause, the
firing continued as Tames Horses poured a steady
fusillade into the cave.

Head down, Hawk raced along the ledge and flung
himself into the cave's entrance just as Tames Horses
stopped firing. Once inside, Hawk pulled up, dismayed.
Gar was sitting cross-legged in the center of the cave
in a pool of his own blood. His only weapon was a
knife, the blade of which he was holding tightly against
the rawhide reata tied to Annabelle. A single, upward
thrust and Annabelle would go plunging to her death.

"Been waitin' fer you," Gar said. "Got yer sister
hangin' out there. Reckon you saw her, all right." He
chuckled, then coughed. Hawk watched with his heart
in his mouth as the knife in Gar's hand resonated
with each spasm.

"What's this all about, Gar? Why you doing this to
Annabelle? Me and Tames Horses saved you and your
pelts."

"Yer sister killed this child, Hawk. And I'm goin' to
finish her. Nice you could come by to watch." His
hand tightened on the knife's grip.

"No, Gar. Don't!"

"She's a tough one. She purely is. A real grizzly."

Gar winced in a sudden spasm of pain and Hawk
saw the steady flow of blood issuing from his vitals and
realized the man was getting weaker by the minute.
His cheeks were hidden completely behind his thick
beard, but his massive brow was as white as marble.
What was astonishing was that Gar had hung on as
long as he had.

"What did she ever do to you, Gar?" Hawk pleaded,
stepping closer. "Let her live."

"No," Gar said heavily, his eyes unnaturally bright. "I'm sendin' her to perdition. She won't be my woman here, so she'll be my woman in hell."

Again Gar's grip tightened on the knife's handle. Hawk flung himself through the air at the huge mountain man. But even as he struck Gar, the knife flashed up, severing the reata. Hawk felt the braided leather slipping past him. Flinging himself about, he snatched up its vanishing tail and just managed to hold on as Annabelle's terrified scream came from below.

Swiftly Hawk swung around to dig in his heels. Winding the reata around his right wrist, he hung on. So intent was he on saving Annabelle he didn't hear Gar moving up behind him. A hot drop of blood slapped the back of his neck. He looked up to see the huge, wavering form of Gar Trimm looming over him.

Gar was holding an ax in his right hand. Slowly, meanly, Gar raised the ax over his head. Unable to move, his right hand clinging to the reata holding Annabelle, Hawk knew he could not reach back for his throwing knife with his left hand and that, even if he could, this close and with such a giant of a man, it would be useless. There was nothing he could do, he realized, and with a fatalistic shrug, he began pulling up Annabelle as swiftly as he could, bracing himself for the blow he knew, was coming.

Tames Horses appeared in the cave's entrance, Hawk's rifle in his hand. He fired. The round slammed into Gar's chest, staggering him momentarily. Dropping his ax, Gar managed to stay upright; he drew his knife and, uttering a roar as shattering as that of a grizzly, charged the Indian. Tames Horses waited, crouching. Gar was almost on him before the old warrior did a quick dance out of Gar's path. Like a wounded bear that did not yet know it was dead, Gar rushed blindly on and with a great, anguished howl plunged out into space, and vanished.

Scrambling to his feet, Hawk finished hauling Annabelle back up into the cave. In a moment he had cut her loose and she was in his arms.

"Jed!" she whispered hoarsely. "Is it you, really?"

"It's me, Annabelle."

"Then it's over now."

Hawk nodded. "Yes."

"I stabbed Gar . . . tried to kill him. But he was so enraged . . . and hurt, like a wild little boy!" She shuddered and Hawk held her for a few moments longer to quiet her, to convince her that her nightmare was finally at an end. For him, the feel of her in his arms filled him with a sweet, sober joy that lifted a great darkness from his soul.

At last she pushed gently away from him, smiled wanly at Tames Horses, as if to apologize for this show of weakness, then looked back at Hawk.

"Brad was here earlier. Gar caught him . . ."

To the question in her eyes, Hawk nodded solemnly. "Brad's dead. Or so near it, he might as well be. He was hurt fearfully."

She nodded unhappily, having already concluded this from what she had seen. "That poor man. He just didn't understand . . . about Gar, about this wilderness."

"He very brave man," Tames Horses said. "He bad hurt, but still he ride and tell us where you are."

"That's right, Annabelle," said Hawk. "If he hadn't, we wouldn't have got here when we did. Gar would have died from his wound and dying, he would have cut that reata."

She straightened then and seemed to shake off all

of it. She was, after all, Hawk's sister, and she had had to deal with death and privation before, from the moment so many years ago when she and her brother had been taken captive by the Comanche. Seeing the iron will now flashing from her eyes, Hawk felt only admiration. He realized then that she had been an equal match for Gar Trimm. In the end, it was she who had ended the wild mountain man's tortured existence.

And for that, Hawk knew, Annabelle would take a certain sad pride with her for all the rest of her years.

— 12 —

Captain James Merriwether and the other members of the U.S. government's newly organized Corps of Topographical engineers returned to Fort Hall three weeks after Annabelle returned with Hawk. During the intervening weeks, Annabelle had managed to fill out beautifully and to banish finally the look of haunting sadness that sometimes fell over her for days at a time. After all, in this outpost she was among friends who did not blame her for her ordeal and who admired and respected her for her courage and beauty.

The captain's joy at finding Annabelle safe and sound was such that Hamilton Walsh decided that the only way to properly celebrate the occasion was to throw a party.

The factor spared no expense and during the party Merriwether, eagerly relating to all who would listen the wonders of California, announced that he and Annabelle would be going on to that sunlit Eden. A Spanish landowner had offered the captain a fifty-square-mile tract of land if he would settle there and bring in fifty families, composed of varying mechanics and artisans willing to settle and prosper in California.

After discussing the matter with Annabelle, Merriwether had decided to accept this most generous offer. Indeed, as he acknowledged to all those about him, he would be a fool not to. This announcement brought on an enthusiastic round of toasts and prompted Joe Meek to propose to the mountain men present that after they turned in their beaver traps and buried their scent bottles for the last time, they should go visit the captain and his lovely wife in California.

This proposal Merriwether and Annabelle promptly seconded.

The talk then turned to California, a land where the sun shone eternally, its inhabitants enjoying a climate so salubrious that Joe Meek had almost refused to return with Merriwether's expedition. The surveying party's time there had been spent most pleasantly, for a week did not go by, it seemed, when there wasn't a fiesta of some kind, or a wedding, or a feast. During their stay they had witnessed bull-roping contests and bear fights, had soaked their feet in salt water, and basked half-naked in the warm California sun. Nor did they neglect their mission. Unable to survey a new route to the Oregon Territory, they had done just as well by verifying that the Humbolt was the swiftest and most expeditious route to California.

As the evening wore on, it seemed to Hawk that there were only very few who did not wish to leave these high cold mountains and move on to California, a lotus land that Captain Merriwether swore would soon beckon to every inhabitant of the planet.

Tired at last of all the talk of California, Hawk and Ana Dolores left the party and went up to their room.

"Sometimes, even now," she murmured, "I still can't believe you're back." She leaned close to him, her cheek resting on his chest.

He ran his hands through her long, silken hair. The heady perfume of her desire seemed to fill the small room. He turned her face to his and kissed her on the lips. The kiss was long and deep, and after it, she took his hand, led him over to the bed, and pushed him gently down onto it. Then she began to unbutton his shirt. He was able to accomplish this task himself, but tonight he was perfectly content to let her do it for him. The rum had left a pleasant buzz in his head.

"What you think?" Ana Dolores asked. "Will Annabelle and James truly be so happy in California?" She slowly peeled his shirt back off his shoulders.

"Yes," he said. "She didn't like it back east. I know I didn't."

"But what about her husband, James? Do you think he's—"

"You mean, is he going to California because he is shamed by what happened to Annabelle? You think he might be fleeing to California to escape the gossip?"

"It is not nice to say. But that is what I mean."

"I don't think so, Ana Dolores. Not Merriwether. I'm sure he is really taken by California, and I know Annabelle would never be happy back East."

"I am happy, then. For them both. It was terrible, this thing what happened. But now I think the bad time is over."

"I sure hope so."

She was running her hands up and down his chest, lovingly, her warm palms following its hard contours. He slipped out of his pants swiftly and she had her dress unbuttoned almost as fast. As she stepped out of it, he saw she had prepared for this moment. There was nothing under the dress but her.

Pulling her close, he nuzzled her warm breasts and felt

the nipples rising eagerly. Then he drew her belly close to his lips and kissed her, letting the fire of her belly inspire him. She moaned as his lips moved down, and then, with a tiny, kittenish laugh, she joined him on the bed.

Soon all sounds of the party below faded as other, more uninhibited sounds took their place.

The fort was quiet, but Hawk could not sleep. Below in the factor's hall, not a single reveler remained awake. Even the Indians outside the fort had given up. Tames Horses was probably asleep now in the lodge of his old crone. Beside him in the bed, Ana Dolores, her head snuggled deep into a huge feather pillow, was breathing softly, regularly.

Hawk left the bed as quietly as possible so as not to disturb her and padded on naked feet over to the single window. He peered out past the tops of the palisades at the moonlit flat and the river beyond. Across the river loomed pine-carpeted hills, and beyond them, the mountains—dark, jagged ramparts against the night sky. He was gazing upon a wild country he loved despite its terrors . . . or perhaps because of them.

As he realized this, he thought of one no longer with them, a young man filled with youthful idealism, whom some had labeled a fool of a greenhorn. Too late he had found out what this wilderness really meant, and the true nature of the noble savages he was so certain peopled it. In the end one of the wild denizens of this wilderness had killed him, but he had died as brave a man as any Hawk had known. Annabelle had assured him she would never forget Brad Balfour.

And neither would Hawk.